He kissed her and she melted, ready to make love then and there . . .

When their lips separated, he held her a little apart. "Your father's in deep trouble. You want me to help him."

"I didn't say that," she answered cautiously.

"Is it true or not?"

She countered with her own question. "Can you help him?"

"Yes."

Fallon walked away from Colby the few steps to the oak and sat down. He followed and stood looking down at her. "I want you to marry Jeff," he said calmly.

Her eyes flashed. "I'd rather marry you."

Colby smiled. "That's very sweet, but you and I have other reasons for what we do beyond what we want for ourselves."

"I wouldn't be any good for Jeff," she told him honestly.

"He adores you. I want him to settle down with someone smart, smarter than he is, even brilliant. That's you, Fallon. If Jeff became your family, you could help him."

"And in exchange you'd bail out my father."

"Exactly."

Dynasty

Starring
John Forsythe
Linda Evens
Pamela Sue Martin
John James
Lee Bergere

Created by Richard & Esther Shapiro

Supervising Producer
E. Duke Vincent

Executive Producers
Aaron Spelling
Douglas S. Cramer
and
Richard & Esther Shapiro

A Richard and Esther Shapiro Production
in Association with Aaron Spelling Productions

3-Hour Pilot & 1st Episode Written by
Richard & Esther Shapiro

Episode #2
Story by Chester Krumholz
Teleplay by Edward de Blasio & Chester Krumholz

Episode #3
Teleplay by Chester Krumholz
Story by Richard Shapiro & Chester Krumholz

Episode #4
Teleplay by Edward de Blasio & Norman Katkov
Story by Richard Shapiro

Episodes #5, #6, #7, #8, and #9
Written by Edward de Blasio

Episode #10
Written by Edward de Blasio and Richard Shapiro

Episode #11
Written by Edward de Blasio

DYNASTY

Created by
Richard & Esther Shapiro

A Novel by
Eileen Lottman

A Richard and Esther Shapiro Production
In Association with Aaron Spelling Productions

BANTAM BOOKS
TORONTO · NEW YORK · LONDON · SYDNEY

DYNASTY
A Bantam Book / October 1983

Created by Richard & Esther Shapiro
A Richard and Esther Shapiro Production
In Association with
Aaron Spelling Productions, Inc.

Three-hour pilot and first episode written by Richard & Esther Shapiro
Episode #2:   *Story by Chester Krumholz*
                 Teleplay by Edward De Blasio & Chester Krumholz
Episode #3:   *Teleplay by Chester Krumholz*
                 Story by Richard Shapiro & Chester Krumholz
Episode #4:   *Teleplay by Edward De Blasio & Norman Katkov*
                 Story by Richard Shapiro
Episode #5, #6, #7, #8, and #9:
                 Written by Edward De Blasio
Episode #10: Written by Edward De Blasio and Richard Shapiro
Episode #11: Written by Edward De Blasio

ISBN 0-553-23352-1

Published simultaneously in the United States and Canada

Bantam Books are published by Bantam Books, Inc. Its trade-
mark, consisting of the words ''Bantam Books'' and the por-
trayal of a rooster, is Registered in U.S. Patent and Trademark
Office and in other countries. Marca Registrada. Bantam
Books, Inc., 666 Fifth Avenue, New York, New York 10103.

PRINTED IN THE UNITED STATES OF AMERICA

H   0 9 8 7 6 5 4 3 2 1

To the Farmingville dynasty:
the trombonists, the
small dancer, the great cook,
the soccer player, and the liberated
computer maven whose many
generosities made this book so much fun
to write

1

"It's the hardest shower gift I've ever bought," Doris muttered as she tied the last pompon onto the turned-up red umbrella filled with packages. "What do you get for someone who's about to marry two hundred million dollars? Nothing for the kitchen, that's for sure."

"I got her a tennis racket," one of the other women from the office murmured. "Do you think that was okay?"

"Terrific idea," Doris answered halfheartedly. She skirted the table, which was opened to its full two-leaf width, taking up most of the room in the studio apartment. Crepe-paper banners hung from the ceiling, taped to the corners of the table to encircle a huge sheet cake that was frosted with a comical bride and groom about to ride away in a jalopy with candy tin cans tied to it.

"Anyway," Doris went on mournfully, "it feels more like a wake than a wedding shower. Who wants to celebrate when you're about to lose a friend forever?"

Charlotte turned from the window where she had been posted to watch for Krystle's car. "That's not true," she scolded gently. "Krystle's not going to change just because she's married to Blake Carrington."

"She won't mean to, but she will." The quiet voice of authority came from the office supervisor, who was

1

older than the others and had worked for Denver-Carrington longer than anyone there. It was respect as much as surprise at her words that commanded the attention of the six other women in the room. "She's the nicest person I've ever known," Mrs. Perkins went on, "but once she's living in that mansion up on the mountain side, her life won't be her own to decide. Her whole world is going to change, and she's going to have to change with it."

"Krystle won't abandon her old friends!" Charlotte protested, and then she turned back to her vigil, spotting Krystle Jennings' blue Mercedes turning into the block. "Here she comes! Quick, everyone!"

A stunning, warm-eyed, slender woman in her early thirties with shining streak-blonde hair gently curving to her shoulders opened the door of her apartment to be greeted by warm shouts and hugs and the happy babble of good wishes.

"But—how did you know I'd be coming home this afternoon? I have so many things I should be doing..." she said in honest amazement after the first excitement had passed, the first toasts had been drunk, and the chatter had subsided. The seven women were clustered around the inverted umbrella on the floor, waiting for Krystle to begin opening her gifts.

"I told Mr. Carrington that it was his responsibility to see that you got here at two o'clock, and not before," Doris said with a giggle. "He looked real stern; you know how he does sometimes when he's about to bawl you out for something. Oh, excuse me, Krystle—well, what the hell, you've been his secretary for a year, and you know what I'm talking about, right? Even if you are engaged to him now—anyway, he didn't much like me telling him what to do, you better believe it, but he caught on right away, and his face broke out in a big smile because it was for Krystle, you know, and he said he'd take care of the matter. I think he really loves you, Krystle. Here's to you!"

They all drank more champagne and laughed, and then she opened her gifts, so terribly touched by each and every one that there were tears in her eyes even as she laughed at the silly underwear, took a tentative, untutored swing with the tennis racket, promised to use the riding crop on the horses and not the servants, glanced at some of the pictures in *The Joy of Sex*, and tackled the intricate wrappings of a large blue-ribboned box from Charlotte. Everyone gasped as she held up an exquisitely beautiful, handmade, old-fashioned silk and lace patchwork quilt.

She was nearly speechless. "You must have worked—months on this!" she exclaimed.

Charlotte tried to make light of it, but she was having a hard time with her feelings. "Six," she admitted jokingly, "but who's counting?"

"All those weekends when you were too busy to go to the movies or out to dinner, you were working on this—for me?"

Charlotte shrugged.

"Oh, Charlotte!" Krystle leaned over to hug her friend, with the lovely quilt spread around their feet. She was out of words.

Embarrassed and deeply pleased, Charlotte hugged her back. "Hey," she said, "you gave me bed and board when I moved out on Bill and had no place to go. My whole life was falling apart, and you took me in. I won't forget that, not ever."

"All of you," Krystle said, "you take my breath away. You're the best friends anybody ever—I mean—this party and—well, I'll never—I won't—ever—well, you know what I mean!"

Charlotte spoke quickly. "You get tears on that quilt, Krystle, I'll punch out your lights! Now, come on, let's get back to the presents. Here, open this one."

Suddenly, the doorbell rang. Charlotte, sitting closest, opened the door. A handsome young man stood there in chauffeur's uniform. The chatter and laughter in the room came to an abrupt halt as he smiled and touched his cap.

"Hello, Michael," Krystle said. She was surprised and a bit flustered at his sudden presence here.

"Miss Jennings," Michael said, "Mr. Carrington would like you to have this with his compliments." He handed her a small package.

"He sent you?"

"He's waiting for me in the car. He knows this party is strictly for ladies," Michael said with a grin.

Krystle moved toward the window, where Marian was already leaning out to peer at the long black limousine below. "He's gorgeous." Marian sighed.

The three women who worked with Krystle in Blake Carrington's office merely smiled; they knew that already. But Krystle's other friends were crowding to see.

"Hey, Krystle, you want to trade?" Alice offered. "I'll give you Marvin, the kids, and I'll toss in six months free diaper service. What do you say?"

"Gorgeous, that's what I'd say," Marian repeated dreamily. "I'd take him even if he didn't have that car and the biggest house in Colorado and his own football team. . . ."

"Well, I think he's the lucky one, to be getting Krystle," Charlotte said loyally.

"Let me take a look," Margaret said. "Closest I ever got to him was when he drove through our picket line during the refinery strike."

They watched as Michael left the building and opened the car door, settling himself into the driver's seat. Blake Carrington, silver-gray-haired, handsome as a movie star, was smiling up at them all, but his eyes and the small kiss he blew with a wave of his hand were strictly for Krystle.

For a minute, she wished he had come upstairs himself, instead of sending Michael. But of course, men weren't allowed at bridal showers—as soon as the thought entered her head, she had to smile to herself. Blake Carrington was not a man who played by other people's rules. If that were true, he'd never have pulled himself up single-handedly to the top of the oil business.

Blake had started out with nothing, the son of a minister who had died quite young, overburdened and unprotesting. The son had vowed to his grieving mother that he'd never live in righteous poverty, never be dependent on the good will of others for his livelihood. So-driven, he worked his way through high school and the Colorado School of Mines, where Blake made himself tougher and shrewder than most. Once out in the world, he was not above marrying a socially prominent woman which he knew would improve his position in important circles; and when their marriage had lost its importance to them both, Blake had generously pensioned Alexis off to live out her days in Europe. His children were grown now, and the only thing in the world he wanted was for Krystle Jennings to belong to him, to marry him. She thought of his kind, intelligent eyes and believed herself the luckiest woman in the world.

"Hey, let's see what the boss gave her for a shower gift!"

All attention flew to the little white leather box that Krystle was opening with nervous fingers.

"Probably a gold-plated time card," Alice started to say when a pair of five-carat diamond earrings emerged, as fiery as the sun, from a soft-blue-satin case.

After a moment of awed silence, everyone began to talk at once:

"Krystle, they're beautiful...."

"My God, they must weigh a pound apiece...."

"Try them on, Krystle, try them on...."

"I've never seen anything so—"

"Well, she sure wouldn't have got diamonds from the other one—from Matthew Blaisdel!"

An instant pall fell over the room at Doris' tactless and unexpectedly loud remark. Krystle stopped, frozen, one earring on and the other in her hand. She was barely breathing. No one said a word for a long, painful moment.

"Doris," Mrs. Perkins said softly, "sometimes you have the tact of a rhinoceros."

"I'm sorry," Doris muttered. "I guess it's just—well, call it jealousy, okay? No, hell, it's more than that. I want you to have it all, Krystle. Honest I do. But I just don't think we're gonna see much of you anymore, and—well, I do wish you'd married Matthew instead, I really do. Then we could still be friends."

"We'll still be friends," Krystle said quietly. "I won't change, Doris."

"I'm sorry," Doris said again.

"Anyway, Matthew is married, and everyone knows it, so shut up, Doris," Charlotte snapped.

"It's okay," Krystle said. "Everyone knows about Matthew and me, I guess. But it's over, way over. I'm in love with Blake, and Matthew is in Saudi Arabia, and his wife is—anyway, who doesn't have something in her past she'd rather not think about anymore? What do you say we cut the cake?"

Reminded of why they were there, the party givers were also reminded of why they loved Krystle and what it was about her—besides her extraordinary beauty—that had charmed and conquered the biggest man in Colorado.

An hour or so later, the party had broken up, and nothing was left except the dirty dishes and wine glasses, ash trays, and mounds of wrapping paper and empty gift boxes. Krystle had turned down all offers to stay and help clean up. She really needed a moment or two alone; doing dishes was good therapy for prenuptial jitters, she figured. There was so much to think about, so many details to attend to.

She looked at her watch and realized she was already late for her appointment with the wedding consultant. The tidying up would wait. She splashed some cold water on her face, put on a bit of lipstick, and decided not to change out of her serviceable blue turtleneck sweater dress. She sped off in the blue Mercedes—down her street onto the wide boulevard that would take her to the mountain road winding up and up to the Carrington estate and its huge electronically locked gates that had recently been programed to swing open at her approach.

She left her car in the sweeping oval driveway,

knowing that it would be garaged and discreetly polished and then brought around again at precisely the moment when she was ready for it. The butler opened the front door before she raised her hand to ring.

"Good afternoon, Miss Jennings. Mr. Afferton is waiting for you in the ballroom," he said, not smiling. She wondered if he ever smiled.

"Thank you," she said, hurrying past him into the bright baronial entry hall with its Roman statues and tapestries and priceless antique tables, sideboards, and chairs. She hurried down the long corridor. The curving staircase rose gracefully from her left as she neared the huge double doors of the ballroom.

Mr. Afferton was pacing the gleaming hardwood floor with his clipboard and pen, frowning slightly.

"I'm sorry I'm late," she said.

He looked at his watch. Behind him, the sun was beginning to turn the sky orange through the trees that shadowed all the rows of wide glass doors that made up the three outer walls of this great room. "I've been waiting for twenty minutes," he said. "Shall we start in here?"

He walked away from her without waiting for an answer, and she followed. He obviously knew exactly what he was about; for her part, she was not only ill at ease in this grand ballroom, the entire house intimidated her. Here she was, planning a major social event for the elite of Denver society, when she still wasn't sure half the time which fork to use for fish and not really convinced that it mattered, either.

"We'll fill all of the fireplaces with flowers," Mr. Afferton was telling her as he jotted something down in his notes. "White Stephanotis, pink tea roses, and of course, pink rhododendrons. Then along this wall we'll build an altar of flowers." He waited for her response, but she was idly wondering what a fireplace filled with flowers would cost. "You do like Stephanotis, Miss Jennings?"

She wasn't sure she could tell a Stephanotis from a tumbleweed. But she would learn. "Yes, of course," she said. Her voice, always low and husky, was almost inaudible in this huge room.

"Unless there's something else you prefer?" He waited for an answer. In his stiff collar and proper tie, Mr. Afferton looked out of place in this sunset-flushed grand ballroom. She wondered if she did, too.

"No, that's fine," she said politely. Just wedding jitters; everybody gets them, perfectly normal."

"I agree. That combination always brings a certain understated elegance," Mr. Afferton said. He moved across the room with quick, light steps, leaving Krystle to scurry after him. "You will enter through that door," he said, pointing with his pencil, "and come down a center aisle, here. Now, which music will you prefer?"

"Well . . . the 'Wedding March,'" Krystle said.

"The 'Wedding March,'" he repeated, looking almost pained. "Which one, the Mendelssohn or the Wagner?"

She'd never make it. Why had she agreed to marry Blake? She couldn't—but a sudden memory of gentle kisses and his face, smiling warmly, reminded her. She looked Mr. Afferton squarely in the eye. "Is one better than the other?" she asked.

"Neither is very *au courant*," he answered haughtily.

Another voice startled them both. "I think what Miss

Jennings actually had in mind was something a little more obscure." A young man was standing in the doorway behind them.

He had an open, pleasant face. He was in his early twenties, with a shock of yellow hair falling over his forehead and a sardonic smile on his face. He entered the room with authority, as if he belonged there. Of course, it must be Steven, Blake's son, just arrived from New York for the wedding. He kept talking to Mr. Afferton as he strode across the gleaming parquet toward them.

"Maybe something for woodwinds," he said pleasantly. "Say Bach's *Siciliana* from his Flute Sonata in E Flat Major. You do know it, don't you, Mr. Afferton?"

Mr. Afferton clearly did not. It was hard for Krystle to keep from smiling at his discomfort, instantly rearranged into a thoughtful pucker as he stammered, "Yes, I do. I do seem to recall—"

Steven pointedly turned away from him and grinned warmly at Krystle. He put an arm around her shoulders and moved with her through the ballroom door into the adjoining music room, leaving Mr. Afferton to follow.

"And out in the garden, a wonderful old harp. And a viola, and cello—how do you feel about that, Krystle?" he was asking her as the officious little man scurried behind them.

"Lovely," she agreed. "Perfect. Thank you, Steven. And welcome home."

He looked at her with a direct gaze that seemed to be suddenly very vulnerable and needy. It flustered her. He had just come to her rescue, and yet he was only a young boy, twenty-two. But he had been on his own in New York for a year, and she had been thinking of any

possible stepmothering problems only in connection
with Steven's sister, Fallon. It was only a split second,
but she knew that Steven was in trouble. He looked
away, tossing out a careless-sounding comment that she
couldn't quite hear. Something about his father's not
bothering to welcome him? She must have heard wrong.

"You must be tired," he said now. "Why don't you go
on and rest? I'll bet I know what you want, and I'll
finish with Mr. Afferton for you if you like. You can
always make changes later."

Krystle nodded gratefully, leaned up to kiss Steven's
cheek, and left the room. Mr. Afferton insinuated himself at Steven's elbow quickly. "She does seem a bit
rattled, doesn't she," he said conspiratorially. "Well,
some of them just can't seem to handle it."

"Handle what, Afferton?" Steven said. There was
danger in his apparently pleasant response, but the
wedding consultant was not shrewd enough to pick up
on it.

"Oh, you know, Mr. Carrington," he said. "The
transition—dealing with—upper-class ways."

Steven's voice was now cold enough for anyone to
feel the chill. "You will beg Miss Jennings' pardon," he
said, "and you will never say or think an insult like that
again within fifty miles of her, or I will personally see to
it that you never work anything bigger than a cat show.
Do you get my meaning?"

Mr. Afferton gulped.

"Good," the slim young man said, nodding and leading the way back to the ballroom. "Now, what's next?"

"Serving arrangements. Sir," said Mr. Afferton, his
eyes on his clipboard.

Krystle had stopped working as Blake's executive

secretary when their engagement was announced, but there were days when her replacement just wouldn't do and he needed her for crucial, confidential work. Krystle suspected—and he would have laughingly agreed—that he simply missed her presence in his office and drummed up excuses to get her back. But she enjoyed working, loved the sense that he truly needed her, and found the office an island of efficient, organized pressure in the midst of the chaos that seemed inevitably to precede a wedding. And so when Blake asked her to come in the following afternoon, she suspected nothing amiss.

She worked at his side for several hours, clearing up the intricacies of a lease on a new oil field in Texas, arranging for translation of a contract from Arabic into four languages so that his international partners and he could discuss it on a telephone conference call the following day, and setting up a dinner in Washington two days hence with two senators and some congressmen to discuss a key piece of legislation affecting his offshore rigs. The time flew; suddenly, it was nearly four o'clock, and she had to dash.

"I've got to get to the dressmaker's for a fitting or I'll be getting married with pins in my seams." She laughed, blowing him a kiss from the door of his private office. "See you at dinner." Blake looked at his watch, smiled up at her, and returned the kiss across the vast mahogany-paneled room.

She pulled on the luscious lynx jacket Blake had given her for Christmas; it still felt strange over her simple silk shirtwaist "working dress." Crossing the reception room, she waved a hurried "so long" to Blake's four secretaries. She was only vaguely aware of the tall, broad-shouldered man who stood across the

room until she felt him staring at her, impelling her to
stop and acknowledge his presence. Her head whirled;
she thought for an instant that she might actually faint.
The familiar face seemed to be a ghost except that his
deep, ruddy, sun-tanned, flesh-and-blood maleness
overpowered the large room, blotting out everything
but the glance between them.

"I didn't know—you were back. Matthew—nobody
told me you—were back."

"I'm back. How are you, Krystle?"

She couldn't answer. They stood there, a few feet
apart, separated by Blake Carrington's plush white carpet,
Blake Carrington's glass coffee table, with Blake Carrington's secretaries watching them and, Krystle suddenly sensed, Blake himself standing at the door to his
private office, watching, too.

She turned to look at him, and he smiled, moving
toward them. Sliding a proprietary hand around Krystle's
waist, kissing her lightly on the cheek, he turned to
Matthew Blaisdel and smiled. "Welcome home, Matt."

Krystle stiffened as a confusion of anger and discomfort rose within her. Was it really possible that Blake
had set this up so that he could observe the unexpected
reunion between herself and her lover? Her ex-lover, of
course, for more than a year now. But evidently Blake
wasn't sure. Could he have ordered Matthew all the
way back to Denver from Saudi Arabia just to spy on
her, to see how she would respond to seeing him again?

"See you at dinner, Krystle," Blake was saying now,
moving with her toward the outer door of his reception
room.

At the dinner table that evening, Blake told her and
Steven and Fallon of the extraordinary circumstances

that had driven Matthew and the rest of the Denver-Carrington crew out of the Middle East. Krystle faulted herself for having doubted him as she listened to the details of a sudden guerrilla attack on the oil rig, trucks burned and exploding grenades chasing them off the field, snipers shooting at them all the way to the airport. Matthew and his coworkers were lucky to be alive.

"I came back on the same plane from New York with Matthew," Steven said. "All he got out with was the clothes he was wearing. A nice guy, Matthew. I like him."

Blake's daughter Fallon looked like a china doll, with huge blue eyes, long curly dark hair, and a milky, innocent-looking mouth. But from those lips more often than not came wry, brittle, even bitter comments. Part of the reason for Fallon's discontent was the natural rivalry that an adored only daughter feels for her father's new young wife, but there was more to Fallon, more depth and intelligence than the spoiled girl was willing to use, most of the time. When it came to business, Krystle knew, Fallon had the interest and keen percep-tions that Blake wished his male child would show.

Fallon was questioning Blake eagerly. "Who were they? Russians?" she asked.

Blake looked at her across the rim of his wine glass, slightly amused at his daughter's eager interest. "Ameri-cans," he said.

"It figures," Fallon said. "What are our chances of getting back in there? Or at least getting the equipment out?"

"Without the marines," Blake answered wryly, "I wouldn't put money on it."

"You make a deal with those people, you'd think they'd keep their end of it," Fallon said, consciously or unconsciously mimicking her father's tone exactly.

"What do you think, Steven?" Blake turned his attention to his son, but with considerably less warmth in his voice.

Steven refused to meet his father's eyes. "I don't know anything about it," he said, not unpleasantly, staring down at his plate.

"Well, don't you think it's about time you showed a little interest?" Blake asked.

"Yes, sir," Steven agreed in a low voice.

"Blake," Krystle said quietly, "Steven has been an enormous help to me with the wedding arrangements. He—"

"Yes," Blake cut in sardonically, "I'm sure he's very good at that sort of thing." But he brightened at the sound of Krystle's voice and seemed glad to have the subject changed. Feeling ignored, Fallon glowered and accidentally knocked her wine glass over onto the crisp white damask tablecloth. When the servant came to wipe it up, Fallon and Steven both took advantage of the flurry to excuse themselves and leave the table.

"Only another two weeks," Blake said, smiling warmly across the table. "It seems forever."

She wanted to ask him, to come right out with it—did you arrange it deliberately for Matthew and me to meet there in front of you that way?—but she pushed the ugly thought away and smiled back. She did love him. It was over between her and Matthew. And he was right; a change of subject was a good idea. There were so many things they should be talking about.

"I wish Fallon felt more comfortable with me," she ventured.

Blake leaned back in his chair and grinned. "Fallon is a bit spoiled," he said. "I know that. But she's a good kid, and she'll come around. How could anybody help but love you? Shall I talk to her? Yes, I'll do that. Tell her how important my two ladies are to me, both of you, and how much I want you to love each other. It's high time Fallon was finding herself a husband; that's her real trouble."

"Maybe it would be better to just give it time," Krystle said.

"No," Blake decided. "I'll talk to her."

His opportunity came unexpectedly the very next day as Michael was driving him and his attorney, Andrew Laird, home from the office. The car entered the gates and began the long roll through the trees that stretched out into parklike gardens on all sides, but neither man looked up from the papers spread on the folding table between them to see the beauty of the grounds or the distant rider on horseback heading their way. When the car phone buzzed, Blake picked it up absently.

"Yes . . . ?"

"Welcome home, Daddy."

"Fallon! Where are you? I'm on my way home." He looked up through the window to find that he was already on his own estate. Then he saw her, only a few feet away, trotting her horse alongside the car. She was talking on a field telephone and grinning down at him as she skillfully, gracefully, posted her lithe body up and down with the movements of the stallion. She was leading Blake's favorite roan, all saddled and bridled.

"Daddy, don't you know there's an energy crisis?

What are you doing driving around in that gas guzzler?" she teased, still talking over the phone wire. Michael slowed the car, watching her appreciatively with side-long glances as he drove.

"Pull up, Michael," Blake said, handing the stack of papers over to Andrew. He loosened his tie. The car stopped. The horses pawed the ground while Blake got out of his limousine and swung easily up into the saddle. Without waiting for him to be settled, Fallon spurred her own horse and galloped off across the wide sweep of grass, ducking low branches and bobbing in and out of the dappled sunlight. Her laughter trailed behind her. In a minute, Blake was galloping after her. She led him a fast and breathless chase, jumping a hedge, cutting erratically through a stand of trees, racing flat out across a meadow, jumping a ravine.

She stayed ahead of him all the way until she slid her horse on his haunches down to the edge of the lake and spurred him to swim across. The horse reared, dumping Fallon into the water headfirst. She came up furiously spitting water and cursing. Blake reined in at the water's edge and prepared to jump down if she needed rescue.

"You all right?" he asked anxiously.

She waded out, dignity in shreds but pride intact. "I'm okay," she said, "but that damned horse won't be when I catch him." She looked up at her father, cover-ing her embarrassment with bravado. "I know you, Blake Carrington. You paid that horse to dump me."

Blake laughed. "I didn't have to pay him. He works for me."

"Is there anybody in Colorado who doesn't work for you?" She grunted, sitting down on the bank to pull off her riding boot. She held it up, and the clear lake water poured out. "Give me your jacket," she said, "and turn around."

"What?"

"Well, I'm certainly not riding all the way back to the house in wet clothes." She grinned, starting to unbutton her shirt. Her father quickly pulled off his jacket, tossed it to her, and turned to admire the view of his private lake and the mountains on every side.

They took the south path back to the house, meandering through flat meadows that skirted the mountain side and afforded frequent glimpses of the city spread out below. They walked side by side, leading their horses. Fallon was barefoot—in fact, bare all over except for her father's dark-blue suit jacket, which hung well below her knees. They talked.

"I've asked Cecil Colby to bring his nephew to the wedding," Blake said casually. But his daughter knew he never said anything that didn't have a purpose. Her antennae began to tingle.

"It's your wedding. Invite anybody you like," she said.

"His name is Jeff. He's bright, and a nice boy; started working for Cecil a couple of months ago. I believe he's about your age."

"I know him, Daddy. We went to summer camp together when we were fourteen."

"Well, I told Cecil you could be sort of Jeff's escort—for the day. He doesn't know many people in Denver yet and—"

"I see," Fallon cut in. "And have you already negotiated the bride price? What are you taking for me—cash or stock options?"

Blake stopped walking. They had reached the bend where the house could be seen, sweeping up from the wide grassy lawn. He looked down at his lovely, unhappy daughter and sighed. He knew how to run corporations and get enemies and friends to do his bidding, but this spirited little creature could get anything she wanted from him. He knew he should be firm with her; he did know what was best, after all. "Fallon, honey, you asked what I wanted for a wedding present. The very best present you could ever give me is to see you—"

"—is to see me happily married and settled down," she finished icily.

"That's right," Blake said.

"That is bull, Daddy, and you know it. Colbyco Oil makes Denver-Carrington look like a corner filling station, and that's eating your liver out. You're not talking about marriage, you're talking about a merger."

His sincerity questioned, Blake's patience ran out, and he answered her angrily. "I want what's best for you, young lady, and yes! I want what's best for Denver-Carrington, too. What's wrong with that?"

Fallon whipped her words at him. "What are you on me for, anyhow? You've got a son; that's the natural line of succession. Let Steven get married; let him provide the royal heir. Or—what about you and Krystle, then? She looks like good solid breeding stock to me."

Blake tugged at his horse's lead and started to walk again. "Oh, hey, I'm sorry if I haven't shown the proper respect," Fallon said sarcastically, catching up to him. "I mean, what would you like me to do? Shall I anoint her feet with holy oil? Or would it be enough for me to kneel down and kiss the hem of her—"

Blake suddenly grabbed his daughter's arm and pulled

her around to face him, violently enough to stop her. His tone was quiet now, but cold and hard enough to frighten even Fallon.

"I am not going to stand here and beg you to accept this lady. You'll just have to take it on faith that she is the most important thing in my life right now. And you and your brother and everybody else around here might as well get used to that."

Jerking her arm away, turning to hide the tears that suddenly filled her eyes, Fallon spat out, "And you don't give a flying damn that she'd rather be in bed with someone else, do you!" She put her naked foot in the stirrup and swung up onto her horse. Then she leaned down for a final jab. "Or do you?" Kicking the horse with her bare heels, she galloped toward the house. Blake watched her for a moment and then mounted his own horse and followed at a brisk, dignified canter.

When he returned to the stable, he was only mildly surprised to see that she had not brought her horse in yet. Out working off steam, probably. He turned his reins over to the stableboy and went in to finish his meeting with the attorney that he had allowed Fallon to interrupt.

But Fallon wasn't galloping over the mountain side to get rid of her anger. She had gone directly to the carriage house and was standing just inside, wearing nothing but her father's jacket, smiling provocatively at the chauffeur. Michael's lean young body was bent over the shiny surface of the big limousine. He was polishing its sleekness with slow, sensual caresses, conscious of Fallon's eyes on him. Without turning around to her, he opened the door of the car, stepped inside, and opened the door of the bar. His movements still slow, deliberate, he took out a small martini shaker, the bottle of gin, the bottle of vermouth, two glasses, and a small silver tray. Carefully, he made the cocktails and placed them on the tray.

When he stepped out of the car, he grinned at her with long familiarity. He came up close and offered her a martini. She shook her head, no. He placed the tray on a tool cabinet nearby and turned back to her with his jaunty smile. "May I take your coat?" he asked slyly. Fallon said nothing, just standing there in her bare feet with her eyes closed, even as her father's jacket fell to the floor of the garage.

2

Alone in her own apartment, wrapped in her cozy lavender robe, Krystle sat down with a cup of coffee and glanced around her with one of those small but satisfying feelings of accomplishment that come from having created order out of chaos. She liked this tiny, efficient nest she had made her home since coming to Denver two years before. When her first marriage broke up, she thought she had lost everything, but she had built a life here, and this tiny room and a half had come to mean independence and security. In a way, she would be sad to leave it.

Without warning, something swept through her very much like terror, a sense of stepping into a vast, unknowable abyss. The coffee tasted sour; she set the cup down carefully, almost dizzy from the overwhelming thought that she might be making the mistake of her life. But—she loved Blake, and he adored her. He was a charming man, thoughtful, intelligent, and caring. The prospect of being mistress of that huge estate was scary—she was sure to make mistakes. Blake had reassured her, and she believed him when he said that nothing she could do would ever, ever embarrass him or make him less than proud of her.

But her hand with the enormous five-carat diamond

engagement ring was trembling. Why did the rather
shabby secondhand furniture and worn rugs in this
walk-up apartment suddenly look so precious to her?
She had heard of wedding jitters; sometimes the bride-
to-be ran away. But she was a grown woman, twenty
years Blake's junior, but still, she had been married
before and knew exactly what she was doing. She was
marrying for love.

It was Matthew who haunted this apartment. Seeing
him this morning brought it all back vividly. His head
on the sofa cushion there. His surprising skill at making
a special salad dressing, scrambled eggs, bringing her
tea in bed that time she had the flu. . . . Matthew
Blaisdel, tall and blond and ruggedly handsome and in
love with her, and she with him. Matthew Blaisdel,
chief engineer for Denver-Carrington, whose salary
went almost entirely to paying the bills for his teenage
daughter's education and his wife's treatment at a mental hospital.

And then he had volunteered to go to Saudi Arabia,
ending the affair that neither of them could resolve.
The wrench of separation and her loneliness had soon
been eased by Blake's attentions—working late, dinner,
theater, concerts, dances, and parties until it was assumed
all over Denver that she was his girl, and then, somehow,
she truly was, and she cared very much for him, very
much indeed. She loved him.

Why, then, was Matthew Blaisdel still haunting her?
It was wrong, dead wrong, and must be ended finally
and forever before her wedding to another man.
Resolutely, Krystle picked up the telephone and dialed
the number she remembered despite herself.

"Could we meet?" she asked simply, and he agreed.

They both knew where to go. She threw on a pair of jeans and a turtleneck sweater and reached into the back of her closet for her tan corduroy jacket. She drove the Mercedes straight out of town onto the mountain highway and up the winding road to a parking area just around a sharp hairpin turn. He was already there, and her heart skipped a beat at the sight of the parked Cherokee waiting for her. He got out of the pickup before she had turned off her ignition and was striding toward her. Krystle acted purely on instinct when she ran into his arms.

Wordlessly, they drew apart without kissing. Slightly embarrassed, even uncomfortable, they smiled like strangers meeting for the first time. Then Matthew put his arm around her shoulders and drew her toward the trail that led down through the brier and rocks to a plateau. From there, the magnificent view of the Rockies all around them against the wide blue sky would put everything—even their unresolved love—into perspective.

"Do you love him?"

"Yes. I mean—I thought I did, until—"

They stared at each other in long and painful accord, remembering the bliss and the hopelessness and the reasons they had been relieved to say good-bye.

Matthew spoke in a tone very much like a private expression of grief, not meant to be overheard. His dear, familiar rumbling voice brought back a rush of sensations that Krystle had long forced out of her memories.

"You've got hold of something good, Krystle. Grab it around the middle and run with it. And don't ever look back."

"But—" Krystle thought of Blake, loving her and counting on her, waiting for her even now. But she looked at Matthew and told the truth. "If I thought there was any way—any way that you and I could work it out without hurting Claudia. Is there, Matthew? Is there a way?"

Matthew avoided her eyes. He looked off into the brilliant greens and blues of the mountain and the snowcaps just beyond. He shook his head. "No. There is no way," he said.

"I know a divorce is out of the question," she said firmly. "But oh, please, look at me, Matthew! I won't marry Blake if you still care for me."

He turned then and looked at her, his eyes blazing. With resolve to lie or with the painful job of being honest? "I don't," he said.

Fighting the devastating hurt she felt, fighting the tears, she faced him squarely. A wall had been thrust up between them, and no matter how she searched his eyes for the truth, she had only his words to go by.

"I'm sorry. I shouldn't have," she said sadly. "I guess there's nothing more to be said."

She turned and began the short climb up to the cars, not seeing the man behind her blink to fight back his own tears.

Matthew's Cherokee kept on going along the other side of the mountain, following the highway toward Aspen. Every time his resolve weakened, thinking of Krystle, he glanced down at the cheerfully wrapped packages on the seat next to him. The card on top was addressed "to Lindsay, from Dad." Deliberately, he banned thoughts of Krystle Jennings from his mind, as he had for the past six months with varying degrees of success. But in Saudi Arabia there had been hard, constantly demanding work to do. Here there was the nearness of Krystle, the misty quality of her eyes only a moment ago, her offering to give up a marriage that would make her the richest woman in the state. For what? Throw her life away on him when he couldn't even offer her a dime-store wedding ring?

He pulled the Cherokee into the driveway of his mother's house. His fourteen-year-old daughter, grown taller and more graceful since he'd been away, came bounding like a fawn across the lawn to throw herself into his arms. She had been waiting, watching for him. Her suitcases were piled in a row on the walkway in front of the house. His mother stood there shading her eyes with her hand, letting the two of them have this moment of reunion together.

After the gifts from Saudi Arabia had been opened and exclaimed over, and his mother's chicken salad, iced tea, and blueberry cobbler had been totally demolished, Matthew and Lindsay kissed Mrs. Blaisdel warmly and climbed into the Cherokee. Waving to her grandmother until they had turned the corner, Lindsay finally settled on her seat and asked, "Where we going now, Dad!"

Conscientiously casual, Matthew answered, "We'll stop and see Mom. Then we'll head back to Denver and get you settled in. Okay?"

The young girl, half child and half woman, was frowning. Her whole face seemed wrapped in a dark cloud as Matthew glanced over at her.

"Honey," he said gently, "you do want to see your mother, don't you?"

He was touched by how badly she lied. "Sure I do," she said, looking straight ahead.

But when he had turned in to the low, rambling

hospital set in its attractive wooded isolation, Lindsay held back. She refused to get out of the car.

"I know your mom would sure like to see you," he said carefully.

"I don't want to go in there." She shrank back.

"Lindsay," Matthew said patiently, "it's a hospital. That's all. And a very pleasant one, as hospitals go."

"It's a hospital for crazy people. I don't want to go in there."

Matthew took a deep, slow breath just to stay easy. "Come on, Lindsay," he said. "You're old enough to understand now. We don't use words like crazy anymore. Your mother had a breakdown. She needed to be in a place where she could get help. She's much better now; the doctor wrote me that she's nearly ready to come home with us, and we'll be a family again. Now that's worth something, isn't it?" *Worth giving up something terribly important*, he added silently to the painful void in his chest. He smiled tenderly at his daughter. "Lindsay, look at me."

Slowly, reluctantly, his daughter turned in the seat to look out at him. He stood at the window, not pleading, only explaining. "Lindsay, this is why I was working out of the country—to get the extra money to pay for this place. It's the only thing in the world that could have kept me away from you. So you might as well come and have a look at it. And—your mother loves you very, very much, and she always has. Don't you think she'd be terribly sad if she thought you didn't want to see her?"

Lindsay tried to smile, but tears overflowed instead. "Please, Daddy," she said, trying not to cry, "don't make me go in there."

He weighed this and agreed. "Okay," he said. "I'll see if Mom can come out—take a little ride with us."

He turned and strode toward the main door of the hospital. But in just a few minutes, he was back, alone.

"Where is she? Isn't she coming?"

"She's gone," Matthew said, coming around to climb up into the driver's seat.

Lindsay froze. "You mean—she escaped?" she whispered.

Matthew found a wry smile in spite of his concern. "Lindsay, I keep telling you, it isn't that kind of place. The doctors felt she was making excellent progress, and so a couple of weeks ago they—well, they let her check herself out."

"Didn't they tell you where she went?"

He took a small piece of note paper from his shirt pocket and handed it to her. "Of course they did. It's just over in the next town. We'll go surprise her, shall we?"

Lindsay's nod was less than enthusiastic.

Claudia Blaisdel was working as a waitress in a coffee shop. In a crisp uniform and comfortable shoes, she looked older than her thirty-one years. Her fair hair was tied back with a simple barrette, and she wore only lipstick. Her face was still pretty; anyone who took the trouble to look would realize that she had once been nearly beautiful. She did not seem surprised to see her husband and daughter when they entered and took a booth at her station.

Claudia finished setting the coffee mugs before the couple in the next booth and came over to them. "Hello, Lindsay," she said quietly. "Hello, Matthew."

"How's the coffee in this place?" Matthew asked in an attempt to set them all at ease. Lindsay was staring down at the table. "You don't seem very surprised to see us," he remarked.

"Dr. Jordan called to tell me you were coming. I'm not terribly good at big surprises just yet," Claudia said, smiling wanly. "I'm awfully glad to see you, Lindsay. I've missed you. You've grown."

"Yes, ma'am."

"Well," Matthew said in the uncomfortable silence. "Well—come on, sit down."

"I shouldn't. I'm working."

"Never mind that," Matthew said a bit sharply. "There's no need for you to go on working here. I'm back. Slide over there, Lindsay. Make room for your mother."

Without looking up, Lindsay slid over, and Claudia sat down next to her.

"So—uh—Dr. Jordan tells me you're doing real well," Matthew said. "You look fine, really. Just fine."

"I'm an outpatient now. I go up there three times a week to see him. I think he'll take me off the medication soon."

"Hey, that's terrific."

Then they had run out of things to say, at least in public. Claudia looked over at the counter where the coffee-shop manager was sitting on his high stool, chewing gum and reading a magazine. Matthew followed her gaze.

"Look," he said, "we can't talk here. Why don't you just tell your boss you're leaving. We'll head on home. Pick up a couple of steaks on the way, some fresh corn, a couple bottles of beer—"

"I can't, Matthew." She looked at him across the

table, her wan eyes seeming to plead for understanding.

"What do you mean?" he asked cautiously.

"I'm not ready. I've got some things to work out. I just can't go on back home as if nothing had happened. Maybe after a couple more months on my own—working, learning what it means to live among people—normal people—again."

Lindsay was rolling her paper napkin into tiny little balls, tight and damp, compulsively tearing bits of the paper and rolling them between her finger tips, lining them up on the table in front of her like bullets.

"It's not only your decision to make, Claudia," Matthew said firmly. "We need you, Lindsay and I. We want you home with us." He waited. Nothing. "Lindsay," he went on with rising irritation, "tell Mom how you feel. Tell her you want her to come home with us now."

Lindsay swallowed visibly, opened her mouth, but nothing came out. Her fingers twitched convulsively at the little pellet she was rolling. It looked as if she might begin to cry.

"Leave her alone, Matthew," Claudia said quietly. "What can you expect from her? The last time she saw me, I was running down the street shrieking about devil worshippers and smashing car windows with a croquet mallet. She has a right to be angry and embarrassed. How would you like to see your mother dragged off by three policemen in a straitjacket, kicking and screaming for all the neighbors to hear?"

"We're a family," Matthew answered. "We belong together."

Claudia looked at him. Whatever memories of anger, arguments, hurts, deceptions, pain, and misunderstandings stood between them, what he said was true. She longed to put her arm around Lindsay, but she could not bear it if her child rejected her, shrugged her away, or shrank from her touch.

"I need time," she said.

She was thinking about how much gray had crept into Matthew's blond hair, streaked from the hot desert sun now the way it always got in summer. There were new lines in his strong square face, too. Around his eyes, from squinting because he always lost his sunglasses, and around his mouth. Those were called laugh lines. She knew she had some, too, now, but not from laughing.

"There may not be time," Matthew was saying with an edge of anger to his controlled voice. "Things are going to happen very fast now for Lindsay. There are going to be changes. Things a mother should be there to explain to her and help her with. Don't you see? I won't be able to do that for her."

Claudia looked over at her daughter, who was obviously wishing she were anywhere else in the whole wide world just now. Impulsively, she reached out to cover Lindsay's hand with her own. "Lindsay?" she asked. "Tell me the truth; either way, it'll be all right, but I do need to know for sure. Do you want me to come home now? Or would you rather have some time, too?"

For the first time since they had come into the café, Linsday looked directly at her mother. Tears erupted and streamed down her cheeks. Unable to speak, she reached for her mother's embrace. They hugged each other, each shaking with her own overflowing emotions.

"Okay," Claudia whispered. "It'll be okay. Everything is going to be all right. No guarantees, but we'll try, won't we? We'll try."

It was only then that Matthew knew with absolute certainty that his decision had been the right one, the only one. He stood up and went to tell the manager that he was taking his wife home.

"I haven't figured out what to do with Matthew Blaisdel yet," Blake Carrington was saying over the phone a day or two later. "The last thing in the world I needed was him back in Denver. Damn those terrorists and their lousy timing. Don't they care anything about my personal life? Well, find something for him in the meantime, will you, Jake—out at the refinery, not in town. Right. I'll let you know when I decide."

He hung up the telephone and switched on the intercom. "Would you ring Miss Jennings for me. I believe she's at home."

"No, she's right here, as a matter of fact," Krystle said from the doorway of his private office. Blake swiveled his chair around to greet her with a happy grin.

"Darling, what a nice surprise. I had no idea you were in the office—"

"I'm sorry, I didn't mean to eavesdrop. I'm so used to just walking right in. I shouldn't any more. I can see there are things in your personal life that maybe your personal friends—and especially your fiancée—shouldn't know."

"What do you mean, Krystle? Come over here so I can see you. What a lovely—"

"Blake, something's been bothering me for a couple of days now, and what you just said on the phone somehow confirms it. . . . My running into Matthew Blaisdel in front of you here wasn't an accident, was it? You deliberately set it up, didn't you? Please don't lie to me."

Krystle was coldly furious. She looked stunning in the simple dark cotton suit she had worn when she first started working for him, and it made Blake remember how he had felt then—that he must have this cool, beautiful potentially warm woman for his own. The unattainable had always challenged him, turned him on irresistibly. In her anger, Krystle was more beautiful than ever.

"Would you believe me if I said it was just a coincidence?" he asked.

Krystle knew he was lying. "No," she said sadly. She turned and walked out of the office.

Later that afternoon, she had taken the telephone off the hook and was trying to concentrate on a novel that should have transported her far from her own troubles. She would read a paragraph and then look around her cozy room and say aloud, "If I have to, I can start all over again. I don't need Matthew Blaisdel or Blake Carrington. I'm just fine on my own. I can go anywhere and do anything I want to and not be dependent on any man's love. . . ." Then she would have to reread the same paragraph, trying to remember the thread of the story. When the doorbell rang, she jumped in surprise.

Opening the door, she was confronted with a solid wall of flowers. Krystle stepped back, and the wall moved inside her apartment. Three delivery boys set down their huge baskets and vases and then stepped out into the hall to return with more. Speechless, Krystle watched her living-dining room fill with flowers— in pots, vases, bowls, baskets, while the delivery boys made more and more trips back and forth. When there was no longer an inch of space in the room, they left, still without a word, closing the door behind them. But almost at once, the bell rang again.

Krystle nearly tripped over an arrangement of roses and anemones in a large silver loving cup when she tried to move around to the door. Blake Carrington stood there this time, his hands behind his back, smiling a contrite, anxious little smile.

"I know I don't deserve to be forgiven," he said. When she started to answer, he held up one hand for her silence and moved past her into the apartment. "Wait, don't say a word," he went on. "I plead guilty to all high crimes and misdeameanors of which I stand charged, and I understand that the very best I can hope for is an executive pardon with loss of all rights and privileges."

"Blake," she said, "this is serious. It's not something I can decide just like that. Overwhelmed by flowers and your goddamned charm. If you don't trust me—"

"I'm just asking you one thing," he said, immediately and irresistibly serious. "Can we talk about it over dinner?"

She was about to say no. "By the way," he went on, "I brought you something."

Did he really think diamonds would change her mind? But the hand he was holding out offered a wilted little bunch of violets. "It's all they had left," he said. "Some love-sick fool bought out the entire store."

She couldn't help smiling, she couldn't resist the look in his eyes, she couldn't help caring for him. Ten minutes later, they were in the car, with Michael driving them somewhere for dinner.

"What would you like to eat?" Blake asked her. "French? Japanese?"

"Nothing fancy," Krystle answered. "And please— nothing expensive."

"Whatever you say." He was smiling at her as though she were a great treasure he had lost and then found again.

"Maybe Chinese," she suggested.

"Did you hear that, Michael?" Blake asked. There was a window between the chauffeur and the back seat, but it was almost never rolled shut. Michael nodded. It occurred to Krystle that the chauffeur was in a position to overhear a great many things; she wondered if Blake was truly aware of his driver as a human being with ears and, possibly, weaknesses. But of course Blake never overlooked anything. Michael must be the most dis- creet young man in the world, or Blake wouldn't trust him so.

But it wasn't the Chinese section of town they were heading for—it turned out to be the airport. Michael rolled the car to a stop on the tarmac near the hangar where Blake kept his Lear jet.

"Blake? What is this?" she asked.

He handed her out of the car. "You'll see. Come on."

They had a drink and hors d'oeuvres aboard the plane and arrived in San Francisco just as the sun was setting behind the Golden Gate Bridge. Blake's pilot had called ahead for a car to meet them, and soon they were in Chinatown, standing in front of a small, dimly lit, unprepossessing restaurant.

"Here we are," Blake said. "Doesn't look like much. But trust me, this place has the best Char Su Bow in

the West." At Krystle's look of pure exasperation, he
shrugged innocently. "It's not expensive. We'll be out of
here for under twenty bucks, including tax and the tip."
He opened the door for her.

"What if I had said French?" she asked.

"We would have had to refuel in New Jersey," he
answered.

The dinner was fun, and not until they were back in
the air on their way home did they turn serious again.
The cabin of the private jet was luxuriously furnished,
half as an office, with a desk, computer, and battery of
direct-line phones to all the world offices of Denver-
Carrington, and half as a comfortable sitting room, with
deep, soft leather chairs and a couch designed as much
to be slept on as sat on. A small but thoroughly
outfitted double bedroom was aft, through a sliding
door. Krystle, shoes off, was curled in one of the big
chairs, and Blake had stripped off his tie and jacket. He
was selecting a bottle from the bar.

"Brandy?"

"No, thank you."

"What would you like?" he asked, checking the tem-
perature of the wine racks.

"My job back," Krystle said quietly.

Blake poured two brandies and came over to stand
near her. "You don't really want to be back where I
found you—typing drilling reports and feeding Xerox
machines."

"I don't see my friends anymore, Blake. They seem—
uncomfortable with me."

He set one of the huge, delicate brandy snifters down
on the little glass table in front of her and sat on the

chair opposite. He leaned forward and spoke very gently.

"They'll get over that. Your friends will always be welcome in our house. You've invited them to the wedding, haven't you? It isn't really that, is it?"

She didn't know what to say. She stared at her hands. The huge ring had turned on her finger, and the diamond was in her palm. Her nails were in good shape now that she hadn't been typing so much.

"Do you want to call off the wedding, Krystle? Is that what you want?"

She didn't—couldn't—answer.

"Okay," Blake said. "Let's do it this way. He took a quarter from the jacket he had slung across the back of his chair. "Heads we get married; tails we don't."

Her head jerked up in surprise, and she stared at him. "You're joking."

But she saw that he was not. "I want you more than anything I've ever wanted, Krystle," he said seriously. "But I'm a high roller. And I'll leave it to fate if you will."

"I don't believe you," she said.

For an answer, Blake flipped the coin. It hit the table, and he clamped his hand over it before either of them could see the result.

"If that says tails under there, we hit the ground and go our separate ways," he said.

She stared at him, chilled but oddly excited, too. Blake started to lift his hand off the coin. She quickly clamped her hand down on top of his, holding it there.

"This decision will affect the rest of our lives," she whispered. "We can't make it on the flip of a coin."

Blake shrugged. "I don't need a quarter to tell me how I feel or what I want to do. I love you, Krystle. I know I want to marry you and spend the rest of my life with you. But I'm willing to leave it to you, or to fate, if you aren't sure. Do you love me?"

"I—of course I do. Yes."

Blake was unconvinced. "A lot?" he persisted. "A little? Forty percent? Sixty-five percent? More than a hurricane? Less than a squall?"

"Oh, Blake, I do love you, but sometimes I feel that I don't really know you at all. You can be completely overwhelming, you know. Sometimes I think I don't even know myself or what I want, really. I've made some wrong choices in the past—a bad marriage, a couple of affairs that seemed good—but I feel a little frightened sometimes when you're being overwhelming, and I look at you and wonder—who is this man I'm marrying?"

Blake's voice was tremulous, on the verge of cracking as he answered her very quietly. "I'm the man who loves you, Krystle, and always will. I swear that. I've built a world for myself where I'm on top. I can have anything I want to go after, but it's only you I want. I started out with nothing, and I had to develop some of the characteristics of certain survivors—the wolverine, for instance, or the shrew or the rattler. Do you know what they have in common? I'll tell you—an abiding contempt for natural enemies. They're afraid of nothing and no one, and they survive. They're not pretty, they don't make good pets, but I have a hunch they need love as much as your domestic short-hair pussycats do."

"Oh, Blake! I do love you—"

"But?"

"Oh, Blake, don't you see? It's not you. It's—I mean, I just can't get used to—"

"Say it. It won't bite you. The money?"

Krystle's hand was still covering his. Neither wanted to break the contact between them. Her trembling fingers caressed the firm, wide back of his hand as she spoke.

"I grew up in a town that was smaller than your dining room," she said. "When my father died, he didn't leave us two hundred dollars to bury him."

"Would you feel more comfortable if I divested myself of all my holdings?" he asked. "Shall I give away every cent I've got?"

"That's ridiculous—"

"Yes, it is, but not because I wouldn't do it. It's ridiculous because it wouldn't make any difference. Because if I were to start from dead scratch tomorrow, I'd have a million dollars by the end of the year and ten million the year after. That's the way it is, but it has nothing to do with who I am. I'm a man in love with you, Krystle." He leaned closer to her, softened his voice. "Do I really have to be poor to turn you on?"

"That's not fair," she whispered hoarsely.

But Blake had come to the end game. He closed his free hand over her wrist and lifted her hand away from him. He lifted his palm and looked at the quarter.

"Tails," he said.

He stood up and turned away from her.

Krystle looked from the coin to Blake's retreating back, and her eyes filled with a mix of terror and fascination. Her emotions were doing triple somersaults on a high wire, and she knew there was no net to catch her.

"Blake," she called softly.

He turned back to her, impassive.

She tried a little smile. "Two out of three?"

He waited, not changing his expression.

"I do love you," she said.

No response.

"A hundred percent," she said. "I swear it."

His eyes softened. He took a step toward her. "Prove
it," he said huskily as he took her in his arms. There
were no more thoughts of Matthew Blaisdel in her
mind that night. A day or two later, she heard that
Matthew's wife was out of the hospital and back at
home; Krystle's only thought was to hope that his
marriage would turn out to be as happy as she believed
her own would surely be.

But patching up a marriage is very different from
launching one. Matthew and Claudia Blaisdel had a
fifteen year history together, starting with an accidental
pregnancy in high school. They had roughed it through
bad times financially, emotionally, and sexually.

There were times when Matthew needed to be alone
to fight his demons in solitude. His old friend Walter
Lankershim found him trying to kill a punching bag in
the gym late one night. Walter had to duck a few
punches himself when he tried to jolly Matthew along,
but finally he got him to come out for a cold beer and
an exciting idea.

"Okay, who was it taught you everything you know
about the oil game, Matt?" said the robust old man as
soon as they had settled into a booth at the bar across
the street from the gym and slugged down the first cold
draft of beer.

"The Colorado School of Mines," Matthew answered wryly.

"I don't mean all that geology hogwash—rock formation and specific gravity and how much of this will displace how much of that," Walter scoffed, wiping a foam from his full gray mustache with the back of his hand. "I mean, who was it taught you how to find oil with your nose? How to catch a whiff of it when it's lying under a thousand feet of rock and all the smart-aleck geophysicists with their magnetometers and their seismographs are punching dry holes in the ground a hundred miles away."

"Okay, you taught me a lot, Walter, but those days are over. I've got a lot of responsibilities and a check coming in every week—"

"Denver-Carrington!" Walter almost spat in disgust. "You think Blake Carrington is going to give anything away no matter how much you earn it? You'll never own a damn thing working for wages, son. I call you son because that's the way I feel about you, Matt, and I'm about to let you in on a piece of the biggest strike I ever—"

"Cut the bullshit, Walter. Not interested. Drink up. I've got to be getting on home."

"Matt, will you listen?" Walter leaned his round, earnest face forward across ths booth and spoke in a low, confidential voice. "I have got rock-solid lease options on fifteen thousand acres out near Meadsburg that absolutely reek of high-gravity crude." The old man sat back, clearly under the impression that he had just delivered himself of a secret worthy of Midas himself.

"Good," Matthew said, downing his beer. "Then all

you need is a hammer and a long nail and it should come squirting up out of the ground like champagne."

Walter's grin didn't fade so much as it slipped off his face. He drank the rest of his beer and set the empty glass down. He looked across at Matthew. "Well, there are a few—minor, you understand, very minor—uh, geological problems."

"Like overthrust?" Matthew asked.

"For one."

"And what about a time lock? Who's panting down your neck? Who's waiting to gobble up your leases when you don't come in on time?"

Walter was incensed. "Do you really think I'd buy up short leases?"

"How much time have you got, Walter? And, by the way, who's tendered the offer?"

"You're a hard man, Matt. All right, cards on the table. I could use another beer, couldn't you? Hey, I know what. Let's get a couple of six-packs and ride out to the rig. I'll show you what I'm talking about, let you smell it for yourself. I need you, Matt. And you need me. Come on."

"I can't, Walter. I'd like to go wildcatting again, but I—I can't."

The waitress came over in response to Walter's signal. Instead of asking for the check as he had meant to, the burly little man glumly ordered two more beers.

"Make it one," Matthew said. "Sorry, Walter, but I've got to be getting on home."

"Maybe later," Walter said, "if you change your mind?"

Matthew threw a bill on the table. "I don't think so, pal," he said.

"Don't count on Blake Carrington to do right by you!" Walter called after him as Matthew left the bar.

"Of course you can count on Blake to do the right thing; you know there's no question of that," Andrew Laird was saying to Krystle the following day. They were in the library of the Carrington house. The lawyer had just taken a stack of papers from his briefcase, saying that there were some technical documents for her to sign, required by the corporation. She would have signed without question, but her stepdaughter-to-be, Fallon, had sauntered into the room in time to hear Andrew's explanation and had snickered audibly.

"He means a premarital agreement," Fallon explained, clearly enjoying Krystle's shocked reaction.

"I'm not sure I understand," Krystle said carefully, and Andrew Laird made the comment that implied she might not trust her fiancé to do the right thing. She took the pen he held out to her.

"It's not very complicated," Fallon said, smirking. "Sort of the rich man's divorce in advance."

Andrew Laird looked up angrily. "I don't think this is a proper occasion for your curious sense of humor, Fallon," he said. "Now, Krystle, if you'll just sign here at the bottom—and over here."

Krystle hesitated. "Don't you think I ought to read this first?"

"Certainly," the attorney said smoothly. He was very sure of himself, as a lawyer ought to be, tall and handsome and wearing suits as well tailored as Blake Carrington's. "If you want to take the time," he went on. "But it's just a formality. There's nothing at all unusual in it."

"Like the Bible," Fallon put in. She leaned herself against the corner of the big desk, enjoying Krystle's discomfort. "You brought nothing into this world, and it is certain you can carry nothing out," she finished with a smirk.

"Fallon, will you leave us, please," Andrew Laird said firmly.

She grinned. "Is that some kind of a hint, Andy? Are you by any chance trying to get me to leave?" Getting no more lively response than a weary sigh, she turned to leave the room, calling back over her shoulder to Krystle. "You might as well sign it, babe. Your wedding won't go on without it, you know!" The door shut behind her silently.

Krystle looked at the attorney. "Is that true?" she asked quietly.

He answered her without hesitating a beat, but without giving anything away, either. "It would be much less complicated for everyone if you were to just sign," he said.

Krystle signed.

Fallon wandered down to the kitchen, as she had always done, ever since she was a baby, for a bit of cheer and comfort from the bustling cook and her helpers. There was always something for her there—a cookie, a smile, a warm hug from the housekeeper or the cook. But this was the day before Blake Carrington's wedding, and no one had time for the daughter of the house just then. Six extra helpers had been put on, and Mr. Afferton was supervising the frosting of the enormous seven-tiered cake under the hands of the French baker who had been flown in from Paris for just this occasion. Fallon got in Mr. Afferton's way and nearly tripped him. She didn't mean to. There just didn't seem to be any place for her.

The baker and the wedding consultant stopped fussing over the cake to consult a large drawing laid out on the pantry table. Fallon looked closely at the cake. Flowers and hearts intermingled with spaces that would be filled with fresh flowers and ice cream hearts the next day. At the top of the topmost tier, a bride and groom stood arm in arm under an arch of spun sugar.

In an instant, Fallon Carrington had whisked the two little figures off the cake and popped the bride into her mouth. She bit off the sugar head with a satisfying snap, letting the body melt in her mouth, and quickly finished off the little groom as well. It would have been much more satisfying if the candy couple hadn't been so sickeningly sweet.

3

Steve was settled back in his old room. Dressing for his father's wedding, he was startled by Joseph's knock on the door.

"Steven, your father would like to see you. He's in the library."

"On his wedding day, Joseph? Wow, I should feel flattered. Imagine him actually taking the time to talk to his son on his wedding day, especially since he's been avoiding me like poison ever since I got home. Did you know he sent Michael to the airport to meet my plane? Only it wasn't me Michael was picking up; it was Matthew Blaisdel, who happened to be on the same flight. I had to take a taxi from the airport. How about that?"

"Your father is waiting for you." Joseph, who had been running this house unflappably since Blake Carrington bought it with his first million, waited like a perfect robot for a more logical response to his message.

"Right. Never keep a busy man waiting. I'm on my way," Steven said shortly. He turned back to the mirror and went on trying to brush down the unruly yellow cowlick that even Mr. Gerard's haircut hadn't been able to tame. As soon as Joseph had left the room, Steven let his hands fall to his sides and stared for a minute at his image in the mirror. He was twenty-two years old; so why did he feel like a kid again, summoned by his father to be reprimanded for overspending his allowance or driving his pony cart too fast?

Andrew Laird was in the library with his father when Steven walked in. Fallon referred to Andrew as the family's *"consigliere,"* a Mafia term that their father did not find amusing. The two men were dressed in their formal clothes for the wedding. They were having a drink at the far end of the mahogany-paneled room. Steven had been almost looking forward to a few minutes alone with his father even if it turned out to be a lecture. *A boy needs his dad,* Steven thought wryly to himself. *How old do you have to get before you give up hoping for the impossible?*

"I'm sorry. I thought you wanted to see me," he said hesitantly.

"I do," his father answered.

Andrew got up from his deep leather chair, set his drink down, and stuffed some papers into his briefcase. "I'll leave you two to talk," he said. He clicked the case shut and spun its combination lock; then, with a half smile for Steven, he left the room.

"Drink?" Blake offered with a vague gesture toward the tray of decanters and crystal glasses on the low table between the couches.

"No, thank you."

"Then let me get right to the point, Steven. You've been out of school for two years now. You have a degree that wouldn't get you a job spraying vegetables in a supermarket—"

"I think I will have a drink, after all," Steven interrupted glumly. He walked over and busied himself with the ice and glass and whiskey.

His father went right on. "You've lived in New York for nearly two years. You've tried to 'find yourself.' Well, son, the search has come to an end."

Steven's sardonic smile was very like his father's. "Really?" he said. "And what have I decided?" He took a long swig of the whiskey, which he really didn't like at all.

"I have decided," his father answered, "that you've been living off this company long enough. It's time you started putting something back. So"—Blake sat back in his chair; the soft, well-bred leather yielding silently to his weight—"as soon as I get back from my honeymoon, you report to work."

Steven put the drink down. It was awful, anyway. "Well, just what career have I picked out at the company?" he asked.

"I thought you might be good at something—well, not exactly strenuous. You might try public relations."

A wide grin flitted across the young man's mouth, but his round blue eyes didn't change. "Public relations!" he hooted. "Dad, do you really want me to tell the public what I think about your business?"

"It's nice to know you think anything about anything," Blake said curtly. "I wasn't aware that you did."

The few sips of liquor and his father's coldness were working on Steven. His bitterness was deep and of long standing, and being out from under for a while had given him some kind of courage that hadn't been tested yet. He had never spoken up to his father, but he was grown now, and he began to realize that he was not afraid anymore.

"How would you know anything about what I do and what I don't do?" he snapped. "Ever since Mother left, I get the feeling you wouldn't quite remember who I was if Joseph didn't remind you discreetly every now and then."

Unmoved, Blake waited for Steven's outburst to be over and then went on with the matter at hand. "About my business, Steven. You had a comment to make?"

"Maybe," Steven muttered. Then he shrugged. *What a waste of energy to get into a hassle with Blake Carrington. No way to win, so drop it. After all, this was supposed to be a happy day for all concerned, right?* "Hey, today's no time to get into all that. I'm sor—"

"On the contrary," his father interrupted. "Today's the day to settle all accounts. Spit it out. Go ahead."

"Okay. Okay," Steven picked up the drink again, but a taste of it didn't help. "I think you sold this country out," he said. His voice wavered a bit, but he went on. "That's what I honestly think. You and Colby and some of the rest of the big oil companies."

Blake poured himself another drink. "Don't stop there. Go on, get it all out," he said, on top of the argument, still handling things.

Steven felt reckless suddenly, almost exhilarated with the sense that he could talk to his father honestly, that whether Blake regarded him as an adult or not didn't really matter. Steven realized in that heady moment that he regarded himself as a man, no longer a scared little boy. He said what had been on his mind for a long time, and it felt good to get it out.

"You didn't develop this country's energy resources when you had the chance," he said. "You developed the

Arabian fields instead, because it was cheaper. You made billionaires of the oil sheiks. Except now the Arabian fields are up for grabs to any army that has the nerve to march in." He stopped, temporarily out of steam and desperately curious to know how his father was reacting.

"And I am personally responsible for World War Three," Blake said unemotionally. "Steven, I've heard this garbage from people I almost respect. Do you really suppose I'm going to take it from you now?"

"Maybe you just don't have an answer," his son replied.

"And what's your answer? Flit here and there for the rest of your life, living off money you haven't earned?" His anger had risen so subtly that Steven wasn't prepared for his wrist to be grabbed tightly and his hand to be turned up and scrutinized. "Your hands are soft as a baby's bottom," his father observed scornfully, not letting go, twisting the flesh and making Steven want to cry out. "Talking about building windmills and harnessing the sun's rays—the most work you've ever done in your life is signing your name to a Diners Club charge." He dropped his son's hand as if it were an unappetizing thing he had picked up by mistake.

Any residual fear of his father was forgotten now in Steven's own rage. "I may not work," he said bitterly, "but at least I don't steal. I don't rob the people of this country by artificially pushing up the price of gasoline!"

Blake answered coldly, on familiar turf now. "That is an allegation that has never been proved by anybody. The Justice Department has said it is not true. The Department of Energy has said it is not true. But my son still believes it."

"Yes, I do."

Blake's anger overtook his coolness now, and his voice rose to a shout. "Well, how in hell can anybody pay any attention to a goddamned faggot!"

Icy silence came over the room. Steven stared at his father, but Blake looked away, regretting his words. "I—I didn't mean for it to come out that way," he said. He finished his drink and went to pour himself another, still fumbling for an apology of sorts. "I didn't mean for it to come out at all, but—well—I had hoped you would come home and go to work and it would all just—go away."

Steven leaned back against the soft leather of his chair. He watched his father's discomfort without emotion, feeling finally and totally cut off. "How'd you find out?" he asked. "Did you hire detectives?"

"I—I found out, that's all. Someone saw you and that fellow you lived with down in Greenwich Village. How could you put your hands on another man? Steven, listen to me. I'm a pretty smart fellow for a capitalist exploiter of the working classes, and when I'm not busy grinding the faces of the poor, I even read a little. I've even read some Freud, and I understand more than you might think I do. I'm not intolerant, Steven, and it will all be forgotten—as long as you try to straighten yourself out now that I'm offering you the chance." It had been very difficult for him to say. He had avoided Steven's steady stare the whole time, but he had said what he needed to, and now he took a long drink of the whiskey as if rewarding himself for an unpleasant job over and done with.

"Straighten myself out?" Steven repeated thoughtfully. "I'm not sure I know what that means. I'm not sure I could if I wanted to. And—I'm not sure I want to."

Blake looked at his son now, stared as though he were seeing some rare and terrible beast in the zoo. He was prevented from saying the hard, brutal words that came to mind by a discreet knock on the door.

"Yes, what is it?" he called out, still glaring hatefully at his son.

The door opened, and Joseph stepped in to announce that the wedding guests were beginning to arrive. Blake nodded. He tossed down his drink and followed the major-domo out of the room without looking back at his son.

The ceremony was brief, the bride radiant in a long white skirt and bead-embroidered jacket. The groom seemed not to have a care in the world, and as they lined up to be greeted and kissed and introduced and congratulated, he even put his arm around his son's shoulders for a photograph or two.

Steven smiled and shook hands and listened to his sister giving their new stepmother sly advice and tips about some of the guests Krystle was meeting for the first time.

"Here comes Jerry Henderson, finest congressman money can buy. And this one is Bradley Milburn, killed his wife three years ago, strangled her with her own panty hose—watch out, he's sure to kiss you. And Andrew Laird of course you know; he's the one who got Milburn off. Oh, oh, the team's here; that's daddy's football team—quarterback, halfback, mattressback. My gosh, who are those women? How did they get in here?"

"Those are my friends from the office and the plant,"

Krystle said serenely. "Margaret, Charlotte, Doris, I want you to meet my—uh—Mr. Carrington's daughter, Fallon, and his son, Steven."

Steven chalked one up for Krystle with secret delight. Then his father was leaning past him to Fallon, introducing her to a good-looking young man with thick dark hair and a nice smile.

"It's really good to see you again, Fallon," Jeff Colby said. "I mean, I've really been looking forward to seeing you again ever since—when was it?—summer camp when we were about fourteen?"

"Yes, I see you finally got the braces off your teeth. And I understand you're in the media relations end now. How's it going?" Fallon asked, obviously not really interested.

"May I take your daughter out of the receiving line, Mr. Carrington?" Jeff asked, and was rewarded with a nod and a pat on the back from the bridegroom. The entire party moved out into the dappled sunlight of the garden where the flute, harp, and string ensemble was playing the lyrical Bach sonata Steven had requested.

Fallon was in a foul mood, although nothing of it showed. Her large blue eyes were clear and ingenuous, framed by the long dark lashes that hid her true feelings if anyone got too close. The dress she had chosen for her father's wedding was a bit daring (to take some of the spotlight from the bride?), but tasteful and an elegant showcase for her slim, perfect figure. Dramatic black crepe with one bright white shoulder and sleeve stood out from the more traditional pastels of the other wedding guests. Fallon and Jeff Colby walked down the soft green lawn past the bar and canapé tables. With champagne glasses and caviar on toast points in both hands, they sauntered near the yellow rose garden to talk. Jeff was doing most of the talking.

"Actually, I'm working on a campaign that I think is going to be really effective," he said. "We're using Br'er Rabbit and the tar baby—that's really directed at American dependence on foreign oil. You see, the tar baby symbolizes—"

"I know what that symbolizes, Jeff," Fallon cut in irritably.

"Yes, of course you do," he said quickly. "I didn't mean to imply—"

She smiled. "Actually, I find it all a little precious."

Like everyone who got hit with the double whammy of Fallon's sweet smile and vicious words, Jeff found himself confused and captivated at the same time. "Precious?" he echoed faintly.

"Lord save me from cute little tar babies and cute little rabbits and cute little oil company apologists," she said swallowing a good-sized draft of champagne. Tilting her head back, she saw Jeff's uncle, Cecil Colby, standing with a group of people nearby. His eyes caught hers, and she knew he had heard what she said. It would be more fun to bait him than this nerd nephew she was supposed to fall for.

"There is such a thing as public opinion, you know," Jeff was saying righteously.

Fallon warmed up to it. She talked loudly enough for Cecil Colby to hear and actually started to enjoy herself. "What have we got to be ashamed of?" she snapped. "That we've worked hard, that we helped build this country? And that we've made an honest dollar in the process?"

Jeff was floundering, bewildered and defensive. "Some people would say a dollar and a half," he ventured.

"Some people also say that America should be divided into collective farms and run by a Politburo." She snapped, aware now of Cecil Colby's definite interest. He had half turned his back on the people he was with. This was her father's greatest rival, and he was listening to her. Heady with the attention of the older, powerful man, she turned all her guns on Jeff, the innocent bystander. "Come on, Jeff, are the oil companies the biggest profit takers in this country?" she asked.

"No, of course not, but—"

"You bet your sweet assets they're not," she said firmly. "Aerospace takes a higher percentage return on equity and capital. So do the television networks. So do drugs and electronics. Why is that such a flaming secret? You want to make this country energy independent—who's going to pay for it? Has the government ever sunk a single well? There ought to be dancing and singing in Washington over oil-company profits. The president ought to throw a party on the White House lawn to celebrate; he ought to invite all the members of Congress and their wives and their mistresses and the page boys and—"

"I'm going to go get myself a glass of hemlock," Jeff put in glumly. "Can I bring you some more champagne?"

"Yes, thank you."

But when Jeff returned, she was gone. And if he had bothered to notice, so was his Uncle Cecil. The two had parried a few words and impulsively gone off together, escaping the wedding and social obligations and Jeff Colby's puppydog eyes.

Fallon was at the wheel of her sports car, accelerating

around the mountain roads, the wind whipping her black curls around her head. Cecil Colby, thirty years older, a man used to taking risks, showed no anxiety at her recklessness, but sat easily, smiling and relaxed. She finally let up on the gas pedal, allowing the sleek, low car to curve effortlessly around the twists and turns of the road. Now that they could hear themselves, Colby looked at her approvingly and paid her his highest compliment.

"You're a bright girl. I expect you'll end up running your father's company one day."

Fallon shrugged and laughed shortly. "Not likely," she answered. "There's an unwritten law at Denver-Carrington. At the upper-management level, there are no blacks, no Jews, no Eskimos, and no women."

Cecil Colby laughed. "Maybe I should give you a company to run," he said. "I'm sure I have a couple of small ones lying around. For you to cut your teeth on 'til you're ready for the bigger stuff, of course."

"You're teasing."

"No, I'm not sure I am. Want to take me up on it and see? What would you like to get into—electronics? Cosmetics?"

She concentrated on the road. "Sorry," she said finally. "I don't take something for nothing."

Cecil Colby leaned back against the red leather and grinned lazily. "Oh, well, maybe we could figure out a way to pay me back someday," he said.

She glanced at him sideways and grinned back. "You're not a bad-looking fellow for a rich old billionaire," she commented.

"Thank you. But I'm not sure that's what I had in mind," he said, laughing.

Fallon slowed the car at a turn-around high on the crest of an overlook mountain and threw the gears into reverse. "I'd better get back to the wedding," she said. "My new mama might be wondering where I am."

But before she had completed the turn, an open jeep whipped past them on its way down in the direction they had come. The driver was either suicidal or in desperate trouble, hunched over the wheel with his foot on the floorboard, hugging the rock-strewn mountain side one minute and careening close to the drop-off edge at every steep turn. Cecil Colby recognized him.

"What the hell—that was Walter Lankershim. What's he in such a rush about—and where's he coming from? His claim is in the other direction. Come on, Fallon. Let's see where he's heading in such a damned hurry."

"You're on!" Fallon agreed, throwing into first gear and taking off with a roar of her powerful engine and a small avalanche of stones thrown up behind her spinning tires.

The jeep was out of sight, but Fallon knew this road well and kept up a manic speed all the way down the steep mountain, taking the turns and curves and hairpin spins with a kind of joy in defying death. At the bottom of the grade where the road opened into the four-lane highway, they spotted the jeep barreling into the clover-leaf that led toward Denver's poshest suburbs, upward again into the mountains.

"Looks like he's heading for your house," Colby shouted over the wind.

"Who is he?" Fallon shouted back. She swerved off the highway and took the curves of the off ramp on two wheels, loving every minute.

"Crazy old coot—he's made and lost more fortunes

than your dad and me together. Knows where the oil is to be found but can't seem to get it working for him. Wonder what the hell he's in such a rush about. Couldn't have a strike this early; he's barely put in his rig."

"Hey, he is going toward our place!" Fallon exclaimed as she turned into the long sweeping road behind the jeep. "Well, the guards won't let him in—"

But even as she spoke, she and Colby saw the gates swing open to allow a caterer's van to leave the property. The jeep, idling in the bend of the road just this side of the gate, rammed through and headed for the house. Outraged now, Fallon accelerated and sped through before the gates slammed silently closed.

The wedding guests had assembled around the front of the house to see the radiant couple off. As Walter Lankershim's jeep came gunning toward the crowd, someone shrieked, and several people scrambled for safety away from the graveled circular driveway onto the grass or the steps leading to the main entrance. There was general chaos and confusion as a rotund, mustachioed man with graying hair and a grease-stained red plain work shirt leaped from the mud-splattered jeep.

Blake Carrington signaled to one of the guards with an almost imperceptible nod. The guard, without for a moment taking his eyes off the intruder, removed a small walkie-talkie from his belt clip and began speaking softly, cryptically into it.

The wedding guests backed off, making a path for Walter Lankershim's furious approach to the bride and groom. Krystle, who had changed into a powder-blue "going-away" suit with rounded satin lapels, still clutched her bridal bouquet, ready to throw it toward her old

friends before stepping into the limousine. Her other
arm was linked through her new husband's, but Andrew
Laird stepped up from behind her and gently pulled
her back, away from Blake, who stood his ground
against the irate, red-faced prospector who came forward shouting.

"I want to talk to you, Blake Carrington!"

Blake met him levelly and spoke softly, but his eyes
were flashing with anger. "Who the hell are you to
interrupt my wedding? Now you get yourself back into
that thing, Walter, and drive on out of here while
you're still able."

Fallon and Cecil Colby had pulled around to the side
of the house, unnoticed in all the excitement, and now
they joined the crowd, hanging on every word of the
confrontation.

Walter Lankershim did not bother to lower his voice.
He was shouting as loudly as he could, and his raunchy,
rackety voice had been sharpened in the rigors of a
hard outdoor life. "You tricked my rig, you son of a
bitch! You put my driller in the hospital. That's got to
be talked about right NOW, and you can stick your
wedding in a dry hole!"

Gasps and murmurs from his guests kept Blake rela-
tively calm. "You're a fool, Walter," he said. "Why
would I want to sabotage your rig?"

The old man wiped the sweat from his mustache with
the sleeve of his plaid shirt. "You want me to go bust so
your lease hounds can grab up my leases," he accused.

Blake shook his head impatiently. "What are you
babbling about? I've got enough to last me three lifetimes.
I don't need your leases."

Behind Blake, his new wife had moved free of the

attorney's protective custody and was listening with
interest. She knew Walter Lankershim's reputation from
her brief years of working for Denver-Carrington. Walter
Lankershim was an oddball, a rough-hewn character
more at home on an oil rig than in society. But he was
an honest man. No one would ever say different. Krystle
leaned forward to hear his accusations.

"When was what you got ever enough for you,
Carrington?" The bitter, angry voice was quieter now.
"You've got the fever just like I do. And it's not even
the money, is it? It's the bringing in; it's the owning.
You won't be happy 'til you're as big as Colby, and
Colby won't be happy 'til he's as big as God, but I'm
going to be bigger than both of you. Because I'm sitting
on a five-thousand-acre pool of forty-eight gravity crude.
And you're not putting your spoon in that no matter
how many of my people you put in the hospital!"

Blake saw Krystle moving toward him, and he managed a tight little smile. "I think my friends are getting
a little bored with this conversation, Walter. If you want
to talk, come inside and we'll talk."

The intruder shook his head. "Anything I've got to
say I can say right out here. I've just come from the
hospital," he shouted angrily. "My head driller got hit
with a four-inch cable; knocked him clean off the rig
'cause it snapped right in two. Five tons of blocks came
down; coulda killed every man on the rig. Somebody
sawed that cable, Carrington!"

"I'm sorry. Accidents happen—"

"You come near me or my people again and I'll—"

The angry tirade was abruptly cut off by a low growl
and the simultaneous attack of two lithe and lethal
Dobermans that leaped from the guards' hold at a

whispered command straight for Walter Lankershim's red shirt. The wedding guests gasped in horror as the man went down under the ferocious weight of the two killer dogs.

The guard whistled once sharply, and the dogs backed off from their victim. Lankershim, more stunned than hurt, sat up, clutching at his torn shirt.

Blake Carrington turned back to his guests. "I apologize for this intrusion," he said. "Walter Lankershim never was an easy man to do business with. Joseph!"

Unruffled and in charge, the major-domo stepped forward. "Yes, sir?"

"What is this, a wedding or a wake?" Blake asked, taking Krystle's arm to lead her back into the house. "I don't hear those musicians playing. Do we need some more champagne brought up from the cellar?"

"I'll have some more brought up at once, Mr. Carrington," Joseph agreed.

"Let's have another toast with our guests, Krystle, before we go. The plane will wait for us." The guests turned to follow Joseph back inside the house. Blake held back just long enough to have a private word with Michael, waiting behind the wheel of the limousine. Gesturing toward Walter Lankershim, who was limping, down but not defeated, back toward his jeep, Blake told his young chauffeur to see that the intruder was made to wait until he could talk with him.

Two people close to Blake Carrington were trying to understand what they had just witnessed. Krystle decided that Lankershim had been looking for someone, anyone, to blame for his own misfortune—when you were on top, everyone tried to pull you down. But Steven knew his father to be capable of anything.

Five minutes later, Steven was on the phone with Matthew Blaisdel.

"Walter Lankershim's a friend of yours, isn't he?" Steven said urgently. "He's busted in here, accused my father of causing an accident at his rig. My father was embarrassed in front of his wedding guests, and he won't take that lightly. Lankershim's still here, Matthew, and I'm afraid someone's going to get hurt unless he gets out of here. Can you come and get him?"

"Right away," Matthew answered. He hung up the phone and turned to his wife. Claudia had been having a bad day of it, not adjusting well to "normal" life. Their daughter Lindsay was being difficult, as all teenagers sometimes are, and Claudia wasn't coping very well. When Matthew got off the phone, he felt a surge of guilty relief at having a good reason to escape the messy kitchen, the sad look on his wife's face.

That damn fool Walter would get himself in trouble as long as there was breath in his raspy old chest. Matthew didn't owe him anything, not anymore, that was for damned sure, he thought as he drove toward Carrington's place. There had been a time when Walter had given him his first job, and there had been times when he had lent Walter money, and there had been times when Walter had blown it all, and there had been times—but all that was in the past. Matthew worked for Carrington now, and Carrington was marrying Krystle today, and because of that damned old fool Walter Lankershim, here he was busting right in on Krystle's wedding day. Matthew thought seriously of strangling Walter as soon as he could get his hands on him.

Steven had left word for the gates to be opened to him, and the Cherokee headed up the wooded drive-

way through the grounds toward the mansion. Spotting
Walter's jeep being towed around the back, Matthew
veered onto the fork in the driveway that led to the
service entrance. Several of the garage doors were
open, and the unmistakable sounds of a fight came
pounding out, loud enough for him to hear over his
heavy-duty engine. Matthew stopped and jumped out.

Carrington's chauffeur and two guards—all considerably younger and theoretically in better physical shape
than the old man—were struggling to hold Walter
Lankershim down. Just as Matthew stepped into the
cool darkness of the garage, he saw a rather badly
battered Walter, shirt torn and nose bloodied, seem to
sag and give in. Caught off guard, the younger men
relaxed their hold on him, and Walter wrenched himself free, coming up from the floor with a two-fisted
body punch that audibly knocked the wind out of one of
the nattily uniformed professional guards.

Matthew waded in, fists flying, punching, slugging,
grabbing, elbowing, and kneeing any way he could to
get the old man free. From the corner of his eye, he
saw Walter's face light up with the pleasure of seeing
him, and the old man seemed to get renewed strength.
They made a damned good team, after all, two against
three and holding their own.

"That's enough. Hold it."

Blake Carrington stood in the doorway, the sun haloing
behind him. When he spoke, Michael and the guards
immediately backed off. Walter and Matthew dusted
themselves off as Blake came over to them. "What are
you doing here, Matt?" he asked quietly.

"Why were they beating on him?" was Matthew
Blaisdel's response.

"He came busting in on my wedding day, threatening and accusing me in front of my guests. He got violent," Blake said. "However, because it is a special day for me and because I am infused with a certain generosity of spirit, I am prepared to overlook your roughneck behavior, Walter, and suggest we discuss this thing as two intelligent businessmen." He ignored Matthew.

"I'm listening," Walter said grudgingly, holding a grimy handkerchief to his bloody nose.

"I made you a decent offer for those leases," Blake said. "But I'm going to up it—three hundred and twenty thousand. Plus two percent carried interest to the casing point of everything the well produces. Which probably won't be anything but swamp gas and dirty water, anyhow."

"Okay," Walter agreed.

Matthew stared at his old friend dumfoundedly. "What do you mean, okay?" he demanded.

"I mean I'm twisted off, and he knows it. Got a ragtag crew that couldn't get oil out of a barrel, because he's sewed up every good hand in the state and passed the word he wouldn't be happy about anybody working for me. And now, with my rig busted up, I'll never beat his lease jumpers. I'm gonna take his money, Matt. At least I'll pay off my expenses."

"Fine," Blake said without emotion. "I'll have my lawyer write you a check today."

"No!" Matthew exclaimed. He turned to Walter. "You can't sell out now. That field could be worth ten times what he's offering you. This is your shot, Walter, and what you've been scratching and scrambling for all your life."

Walter shook his head. "What do you care about that? You're working for him, ain't you?"

Matthew turned to confront Blake Carrington. Their eyes met squarely in the late-afternoon rays that fed through the skylights of the garage. The two men were about the same height, one with elegantly cut silver gray hair, expensively groomed and tailored in his wedding suit, the other square-jawed, sandy-haired, and wearing jeans and boots and an old air force jacket.

"Did you wreck his rig?" Matthew asked Blake Carrington.

Coldly furious at the interference, Blake did not trouble to hide his anger. "If I did or if I didn't, it's none of your business. Your job is to dig where I tell you to dig. That's all."

Matthew nodded thoughtfully. "Then maybe you just ought to take that job and stuff it," he said. "Come on, Walter. We weren't invited to this party, anyway."

All the men in the garage were startled to see Krystle Jennings Carrington standing in the doorway. Matthew hesitated only a second, then held out his hand to his lost love.

"I hope you have a happy life," he said, meaning it.

But as always, Blake Carrington had the last word. "Don't you worry," he said icily. "I'll see to that!"

4

Matthew Blaisdel went out to the rig with Walter Lankershim that same night, and he, too, could almost smell the oil deep below the earth. Suddenly excited, he agreed to go partners, to pull that oil out of the ground without Blake Carrington's money, to find investors somewhere else, to find the workers and the equipment despite the barriers Blake Carrington had put up already and the worse ones he would think of.

Throwing himself into the hard, physical work and the never-ending problems of being his own boss made it impossible for Matthew to dwell on thoughts of the woman he had lost—or the woman he had married. Claudia's sadness hadn't lifted much despite the twice-weekly visits to the psychiatrist and the pills she took. Matthew knew some of it was his fault, that she needed something more than he could give her just now, but there was just so much a man could do even with the best intentions in the world. He couldn't force himself to make love to one woman when another was so much in his heart. . . . Matthew let the new rig and all its problems fill his every waking moment.

And the problems were multiplying. Too many coincidences to be just plain old hard luck. Walter was convinced that Blake Carrington was just waiting to take over, now that he had the second lease. If Carrington had wanted the rig stopped when it was competition, Walter argued, think how hungry he is now that he stands to own it if we fail. But Matthew didn't want to think about Blake Carrington, who was on the other side of the world, taking off and landing in his private jet on whatever Polynesian islands took his fancy, on his idyllic honeymoon.

"Sorry, Matthew, I'm out of the two and seven-eighths tubing. Won't get any more in for a while; couple weeks, anyway."

Matthew had all he could do to hold his temper. It had been nearly a month of frustrations and one problem after another that didn't need to happen, and now old George Gandrey baldly lying to him.

"You tell me you're out of it, but I come down here and find enough for six wells, George. Ours is going to come in, and you know it. So just ship the pipe, okay? You know damned well you'll get paid for it, so what's the problem?"

The old sourdough, baked dry by years in his oil-well supply facility, squirmed and squinted and avoided Matthew's eyes. "I sold your order," he finally said reluctantly. "A big account came in, cash on the line. It's just business, Matthew, nothin' personal."

"A big account. Carrington."

"I never said who," the old man said, fidgeting with his hands dug deep into his loose-fitting jeans.

"No, you didn't, but I did," Matthew answered angrily. "Carrington is in second position on our leases. If we don't bring in our well on time, he takes over. But forget it, George. Why should you take a chance on putting Carrington out for a couple of old friends?"

He started for the Cherokee; before he could get to the fence, George Gandrey called out after him.

"There's a guy downstate calls his place Torres Pipe and Valve. He's got all the pipe you're gonna need. I'll call him for you."

Matthew turned back to Gandry, surprised. The old sourdough shrugged. "I don't have to tell you to forget how you found out, do I?" he added gruffly.

Walter shook the old man's hand and climbed into the car. He drove to the roadside diner where he was meeting his partner. Walter was there already, hunched over a cup of coffee and frowning.

"Okay, I know where we can get the pipe," he said, sliding into the opposite side of the booth.

Walter looked up at him. "Yeah?" He grunted. "What are we going to do with it?"

Matthew laughed. "Bring in the richest field this side of Spindletop. At least that's what you said when you dragged me into this damn-fool operation."

"That was before the crew walked off." Walter grunted.

"Walked off! What happened?"

Walter's eyes were red and tired and old. His hands shook a bit, holding onto the coffee mug, as he talked. "The bank found another reason to stall on our loan application, and when I went back without the payroll, those yahoos we got working for us said so long. They walked off, just like that. Just packed up and didn't even say good-bye. That's what I've always liked about the oil business—the loyalty."

There was nothing Matthew could think of to say to ease the old man's bitterness.

"Let's have lunch," he said, studying the menu so he

wouldn't have to keep on looking at his partner's disappointed face.

That was the very day that Matthew's wife decided to shake herself out of the fears and loneliness she had been living with. In fact, at that very moment, Claudia Blaisdel was driving up to her husband's rig with a cheerful smile on her face and a feeling of triumph because she had driven all the way without panic or trepidation. It was the first time she had dared to drive since her breakdown, and she arrived at the site with a sense that something new might truly begin for her and Matthew now. It was a bright, cloudless day, and the machinery stood oddly still around the half-built well.

She got out of the car, carrying the picnic basket she had prepared with sandwiches and cheese and wine. Shaking off an eerie feeling of ghosts and silences, she headed for the little shed that served as the office. But the door was locked.

"Matthew?" she called tentatively. Her voice echoed across the stretch of sandy terrain toward the foothills and the mountains beyond. "Matthew?" she called again, louder. *I won't be frightened*, she said to herself in the silence.

Something moved. She caught a glimpse of a yellowish head and a pale face that seemed to materialize from below the pipe hole in the middle of the deserted rig. She gasped.

"I'm sorry. I didn't mean to frighten you." The voice was boyish and apologetic. A slim young man in blue shirt and jeans and expensive boots clambered out of the hole and stood shyly waiting for her to say something.

"I—I guess you did, a little," she said, trying to smile. "Where is everybody?"

"I don't know," the young man said. "I'm looking for Matthew Blaisdel."

"So am I," Claudia said. "I'm Mrs. Blaisdel."

He came closer and extended his hand. He had a pleasant, open face and an endearing smile. "I'm Steven Carrington," he said. His hand was firm and felt cool and strong to her. She let him lead her to a makeshift bench, a four-by-four plank set across two low barrels. She sat down.

"I wonder where everybody is?" she said. "I guess out to lunch. This was really dumb of me." She indicated the picnic basket at her feet. "I thought I'd surprise him."

"That's nice," Steven said warmly.

"Do you have any plans for lunch?" she asked impulsively. "I've got wine here—and chicken—"

"I'd sure like to," he said, and she knew he meant it. "But I have to find your husband—matter of business. I guess maybe they'd be at Meadsburg?"

"I guess," she agreed politely.

He started off, then turned around and called back to her, "Can I have a raincheck? I'd really like to sometime. I haven't been on a picnic since I was a little kid."

"Sure," she called back. She ate her festive lunch alone, in the shadow cast by the half-built oil rig.

Steven found Walter and Matthew at the Driller's Bar in Meadsburg, having a few beers with a gang of hard hats from the oil fields. Although it was the middle of the afternoon, no one there seemed to be in any hurry to get back to work. Steven walked in on an arm-wrestling contest between Matthew Blaisdel and a huge, tough-looking hombre named Ed.

"Pin him, Big Ed!" shouted one of the roustabouts. "Show him who's really boss!" General laughter followed this, but there was some cheering on the other side, too. Walter Lankershim, for one, sitting at the bar, pretending nonchalance, cracking peanuts and grunting through his teeth.

"Kill the son of a bitch, Matt—him and the rest of those bums!"

Ed had a hard edge to him and looked like he could be dangerous in a real fight. Strong and fiercely determined, he focused his wiry energy on his arm and fist until it slowly, slowly forced Matthew's to the table.

Matthew stood up and offered his hand to Ed while more beer was ordered all around. Another rigger came up to the table and grinned at Matthew. "How about me next," he said, sneering, "now that you're on a losing streak?"

Steven sat down at the bar and ordered a Coke.

"You're wrong about that, Bobby," Matthew said, smiling. "We've had some bad luck, but we're not losers. Anybody here who doesn't understand that and isn't willing to take a chance ought to be working in a nice safe supermarket somewhere. The oil business is a gamble; that's why we're all in it. So where's your gambling spirit, fellas?"

"Hey, that speech worked the last time, Matt, so save the tears. You don't pay us, we don't work. We like you, Matt, but we don't like you that much."

Walter Lankershim was grumbling to himself at the bar, muttering, "Look at 'em, all of 'em! We cleaned out the jails and the flophouses to give 'em a chance, and now they're ready to stab us in the back for our trouble. Trash! Dregs!"

But his partner was being diplomatic and friendly, and the men in the room were listening to Matthew instead of the old man.

"Tell you what. All of you. I've got some pipe coming, and I think I can get a loan from a new bank over in Pueblo. So come on back to work and you'll still get paid for a full day today." The room was silent. "How about it?" Matthew asked.

No one answered until Steven spoke out, loud and clear. "I'll work for you, Matthew."

Everyone in the place turned to stare. He had never felt so uncomfortable in his life, but he hoped he didn't show it. "Just tell me what to do," he said firmly. "I've been around oil rigs all my life—"

"Aint you Blake Carrington's kid?" someone cut in.

"I'm Steven Carrington," he said, and waited for the response, almost ducking his head to shield himself from imaginary rotten eggs. He had grown up surrounded by his father's enemies as well as his father's money.

"Hey, you know that black stuff that made your daddy rich? It'd take a week to wash it off of you!"

"Yeah, you'd go home stinking of kerosene and gasoline oil. Those nice clothes would get all sweaty."

"Yuch!" The derisive laughter swelled and rippled through the room.

"What's your daddy gonna say if you get that two-hundred-dollar shirt all sweaty?"

"He don't wash it, dummy. He throws it away!"

The man who had arm wrestled Matthew to defeat

stepped forward and faced Steven squarely. He spoke loudly, addressing his cronies but never taking his eyes from Steven's.

"You guys. You don't get it yet. His old man probably sent him over to be his spy." His eyes narrowed and glinted then as he spoke to Steven directly. "We may be rabble and dregs, but your father's the biggest crook who ever lived!"

He stood his ground. The bar went completely silent.

"Go on home, boy," Walter Lankershim said quietly from the bar behind him.

Steven swallowed his fear. "My father is not a crook," he said. He slid off the stool so that he was standing face to face with Big Ed. "He never walked off a job," Steven went on boldly, hoping his voice didn't quake, "and he never let down a friend who was in a jam."

"Well, well." Ed smirked. "Now you told me that, you want to show me?"

Matthew Blaisdel's voice rose from the knot of men who had edged in to see the fight. "I can't help you with this one, Steven," he said. "You either take him or you walk. Your father is not real well loved around here."

Steven hesitated, turned away, and then suddenly turned back and landed a punch on Big Ed's outthrust chin. The roustabout stuck his tongue out, tasted blood, grinned, and lunged at Steven with the brute force of a grizzly bear.

The fight was brief but painful. Ed struck with iron fists and obvious enjoyment, while Steven pounded back as best he could, missing most of the time and leaving himself wide open for blow after blow. One final, neat uppercut to the jaw knocked Steven semi-conscious, off his feet and on the floor. He struggled to get up.

"Hey, kid. Enough," someone said from far above him. It was the old man, Walter, leaning down from his bar stool. "You did good," he said.

Steven got to his knees, shook his head to clear it, and struggled to stand.

"Stay down, will you?" his opponent growled. "Matthew, I don't want to kill the kid; tell him to stay down!"

"Okay, that's enough." Matthew Blaisdel and Walter Lankershim lifted Steven between them and helped him toward the door of the bar, practically carrying him.

"Do I get the job?" he asked through swollen lips and the taste of his own blood.

"Yeah, you got it." Matthew grunted. "That makes three of us."

The bright sun nearly put the young man all the way out. He tried to walk, but his feet wouldn't listen to his bursting head.

"What're you hiring him for?" Walter asked as they made their way toward the jeep

"Well, you've got to admit he showed some grit back there," Matthew answered.

"That doesn't mean—"

"Walter, don't you ever see anything good in anybody? He's not Blake Carrington. He's his own man."

They dumped him in the back seat, not too roughly, and Walter got behind the wheel. As the jeep passed the bar, Big Ed and some of the others signaled for them to slow and stop.

"Okay," Ed called out. "You win, Matt, but if we don't get our money by Friday, that's it."

Walter nodded curtly and threw the jeep in gear again. Matthew smiled, and Steven leaned over the edge of the jeep to throw up.

"My god, what nasty little games have you been playing?" his sister asked when he came home after working out the rest of the afternoon around the rig. Bruises had begun to discolor his face, and his mouth was swollen, with dried blood in the corners. One eye was almost shut and starting to turn dark purple. His shirt was torn, and his corduroy jeans were smeared with dirt and sawdust.

"Tell you all about it as soon as I get a shower," he mumbled, limping toward the stairs.

"I've got news for you, too," Fallon called after him. "The perfect honeymoon has been cut short. Dad and what's-her-name are on their way home. Be here tomorrow morning."

Steven stopped halfway up the staircase. "Why? What's happened?"

Fallon shrugged. "Far as I can gather, it seems there's this little country that has a whole lot of Denver-Carrington money tied up in proven reserves, and they've just assassinated the generalissimo and blockaded all tanker traffic."

"Wheeoo!" Steven whistled. "Good thing I've got myself a job. Don't worry, Fallon, I'll support you if Dad loses it all. I'm getting minimum wage already, and I just started today."

"Hey! You mean—all that grease on you isn't our grease? You're not working at the refinery?"

"Nope. I'm on my own, with a bloody nose and a black eye to prove I earned it, too."

"Father's gonna have a fit," she said.

"Wouldn't be a bit surprised," he agreed, going on up the winding staircase to his rooms.

After dinner, Fallon realized that she was truly worried about the business and about her father's state of mind. Feeling restless and helpless, she phoned Jeff Colby and told him to come over for a tennis game at eight in the morning. She didn't want to be alone and just waiting when her father came home with Krystle Jennings.

"You'll never get any power behind the ball if you don't step into it," Jeff counseled wisely as they changed after the first game.

"Who asked you?" she retorted.

He laughed. "Hey, I don't need to come over here to be insulted. I could go play tennis with my uncle if I wanted that."

"Cecil better than you?" she asked.

"He likes to think so, and I let him," Jeff said.

He kept her running all over the court, easily slamming long, hard passing shots down the line just out of her reach, making her run to the net for volleys and then lobbing the ball in slow, leisurely arcs high over her head, to touch down just on the baseline beyond reach of her racket. Fallon ran forward and back, from one side of the court to another, swinging with perfect form and all her strength, only occasionally making contact with the ball.

"Give up?" he asked as they changed sides again after he had taken the first three games.

"Never! I'll run 'til I drop, but you'll never get the better of me."

He laughed. His serve was nearly an ace, and then something broke his concentration. He took his eyes off the ball just as she hit it back.

"There's the car. They're coming," he said.

She returned the ball low and dirty, right at him. Not ready for it, Jeff had his racket down, and the ball socked into his lower abdomen with the force of Fallon's 110 pounds and all the speed she could give it. Jeff bent over in pain. Contrite, Fallon ran to his side.

"Are you all right? I didn't mean it. I'm sorry."

"Yeah, I'm all right. It's—oof—it'll be okay. I know you're upset. I know you didn't mean it. I'm okay."

Fallon looked past the trees to the long, winding drive. The car was slowly approaching the front entrance of the house. "I'm worried about my father, Jeff," she said, letting her guard down for a rare moment.

"Worried about Blake Carrington?" Jeff joked. "The meanest, toughest, smartest man who ever worked his way up the ladder to gobble up a corporation?"

Fallon refused to be jollied out of her sad mood. "He used to be the toughest," she said, "but he's being distracted by her. The old Blake Carrington would never have been caught with his reserves down. He would have seen it coming and got his tankers out of there—every one of them full, too."

Jeff reached for her hand. He gentled his voice. "He'll get out of this jam the way he's gotten out of everything. And Krystle—"

Fallon pulled her hand away. "What about 'and Krystle'?"

Jeff shrugged. "She's a nice lady," he said. "And she's a beautiful lady. And she'll make him happy. What's so terrible about that?"

The car had disappeared from their view and pulled up at the front entrance now. "She won't be happy 'til she's got him down to her own level," Fallon snapped. "Where she's comfortable."

"That's pretty heavy," Jeff said, a bit embarrassed, not knowing how to soothe her, this girl he absolutely adored. "Come on," he said, "let's go and say hello. At least be civil." Fallon didn't move. "I'll tell you what," Jeff cajoled her, "you come and I'll tell what's wrong—what's really and truly wrong—with your backhand." He smiled, but she refused to smile back. She turned toward the house, and he followed.

Michael was unloading the baggage from the trunk of the limousine. Krystle, with sun-tanned skin and sun-brightened hair falling straight to her shoulders, was dressed in a simple wrap dress of bold Polynesian colors that set off the sparkling blue of her eyes. She was radiant, standing on the threshold with a large polished wood carving in her arms, every hair in place and ready to take over the household. Fallon felt sweaty and grimy after the strenuous workout on the tennis court. She ran forward to throw herself into her father's arms.

"Daddy!"

He put his arms around her. He was glowing, too. She could feel his happiness right through his shirt. "Hello, baby."

She reached up and kissed him, hard, on the corner of his mouth. "Welcome home."

Blake loosened himself from her arms and turned to Jeff Colby, clearly pleased to see him there. "Been taking good care of her, Jeff?" he asked. Fallon could have kicked him.

"I've been trying to, sir," the wimp answered, grinning and reaching out his hand to shake her father's. "It's good to have you back."

Fallon turned to her new stepmother. Krystle was still standing near the door as Michael worked his way past her with load after load of baggage, shopping bags filled with gifts, wrapped packages from shops in Hong Kong and Bali and Bangkok. Joseph stood calmly and politely, as always, directing Michael discreetly and waiting for the party to enter the house.

Fallon looked at the wooden artifact Krystle was holding. "That's very nice," she said dryly. "Maybe you can have it wired as a lamp or something."

"That's an idea," Krystle answered pleasantly. Fallon wondered if she'd gotten the dig and had the uncomfortable feeling for an instant that her stepmother wasn't quite as dumb and vulnerable as she seemed.

Blake took Krystle's arm and with his other hand reached out to guide Jeff inside the house with them. "How's your uncle doing?" he asked genially.

Fallon was the last to step inside the reception hall. The chauffeur reached out his hand to stop her as she started to pass by.

"What are you letting him hang around for?" he whispered angrily.

Fallon looked at him and almost smiled. "Jeff Colby?" she scoffed. "I'm only keeping him around 'til I can beat him in tennis. Then I'll throw him away and get somebody I can't beat."

She brushed past him and went inside.

Her father and Jeff had gone on somewhere, probably into the solarium for coffee. But Fallon was in time to overhear something that delighted her. Krystle was standing at the foot of the staircase in conversation with

Joseph. Fallon sat down on an alcove chair in the
reception hall and blatantly eavesdropped.

"My luggage . . . ?"

"It's been taken to your room, Mrs. Carrington. At
least, I assume it is. I'll have a look."

"Oh, that's not necessary, Joseph! I'm sure that—"

The suave, domineering major-domo interrupted her.
"It's my duty to check, madam, if you feel there is
anything out of order."

Fallon had to move forward toward the tapestry
corner of the reception hall to hear their voices as the
two ascended the staircase.

"Joseph, you're going to have to forgive me. I mean,
I know this house, of course, but I've never lived in this
house. And I'm not used to dealing with servants."

Fallon had to cover her mouth with her hand to keep
from gasping or giggling at that. Joseph must be having
a genuine fit at that one, although, of course, he
wouldn't say anything.

Krystle went on, getting herself in deeper. "I didn't
mean to imply that you're—I mean—I understand that
you're the—the one in charge. The major-domo? Is that
right? Is that the right term, Joseph?"

"That will be fine, Mrs. Carrington." His icy voice
trailed down faintly to Fallon as they rounded the
landing and headed down the upstairs hall, out of her
range.

By the time she had her shower and changed and
came back downstairs to the solarium, Jeff Colby had
gone, and Andrew Laird was there conferring with her
father. Fallon poured herself some coffee and joined
them. They didn't seem to notice her.

"What does the State Department expect me to

do—invade the damned country to get my oil out?"
Blake was saying.

"The secretary says wait and see. Everyone says wait
and see. Everything depends on which of the fanatics
manages to kill off the others and come out on top." The
lawyer shrugged. "Maybe he'll be smart enough to turn
your tankers loose."

Blake shook his head. His silver hair glinted in the
sunlight, and once again Fallon was struck by how
handsome a man her father was. Especially with his
face all tanned from the sun. "Or maybe he'll just
nationalize the whole shooting match and trade it to the
Russians for MIG 21s," he said glumly.

He bit into a Danish pastry from the hot tray and
spread some papers out on the table in front of him.
"What kind of advances can we get while our crude's
tied up?" he asked Laird.

"Twenty cents on the dollar. Maybe."

"Where would that leave us?"

The lawyer shook his head. "Bankruptcy," he said
quietly. "And that's the upside."

Blake put the pastry down, wiped his hands carefully,
thoughtfully. "Six operational offices from Tangiers to
Capetown," he said. "Payoffs to every swindling five
percenter in sight. And we get caught like this. What
dimwitted office boy ever thought up this scheme,
anyhow?" he said ruefully.

Andrew Laird's mouth twitched in what was about as
close as he ever came to a smile. "You, as I recall," he
said.

Fallon couldn't sit quietly another minute. "I still
think it's a good idea," she said. She uncurled herself
from the chair behind them and came over to stand

near her father's chair. Both men looked up at her,
more in surprise than courtesy or genuine interest, but
they seemed to be listening.

"I believe your analogy at the time had to do with the
grasshopper and the ants," she said evenly. "Government
isn't putting anything by for a rainy day, you said.
Maybe Denver-Carrington should. Remember?"

Blake frowned, but fondly. "Fallon, how did you get
in here?"

She hooked a strawberry-filled pastry from the tray.
"I told the guard at the door I was CIA," she said,
biting into it. "Undercover."

"Well, be a good girl and run along," her father said,
turning his attention back to his papers.

"Will you buy me a book of paper dolls? And a new
tea set?" Fallon retorted.

He had tuned her out and answered her automatically.
"Whatever you want, Fallon. I'm busy now."

He got up from his chair and took Andrew Laird by
the arm, walking him away from Fallon toward the
sunlit east end of the room. Lush green plants framed
all the windows, and the white wicker furniture did
nothing to muffle the sound of their voices. Having
dismissed Fallon, her father assumed she was gone.

"While we're waiting and seeing what happens over
there, is there anything else I should know about what's
going on—closer to home, I mean?"

Fallon was interested to note that Laird looked a bit
sheepish, if not embarrassed. She leaned in to hear.

"About the Lankershim-Blaisdel property—we haven't
quite got a hook into that yet," the lawyer said. "We
stop their supplies; they find new sources. We cut off

their money; they get new backing. Every time we slow them down, they—"

"Spare me the petty details, Andrew. Just handle it. Our stockholders aren't going to be very happy if we have nothing to show them on the positive side when this other thing comes crashing down. I want that lease. If your present methods aren't working, perhaps you'd better try—"

"A little Carrington hospitality," Fallon finished for him loudly and clearly.

When her father turned to look at her, annoyed, she was innocently munching on her pastry.

"Fallon, will you please—"

"Okay, okay, I'm going. I'm only trying to say"—having his attention now, she began backing slowly toward the doors—"that you might catch more flies with honey than you are with buttermilk," she went on.

Blake took a threatening step toward her. "You. OUT."

Miserably, Fallon put her hand on the doorknob and spilled the words out as fast as they would come. "Daddy, listen to me. Matthew Blaisdel was your friend once. What would it hurt to invite him into your house like a human being and explain to him the advantages of coming back into the company. And bringing his leases with him."

Was he actually considering what she was suggesting? She pressed her advantage. "Or maybe you're so bloody jealous about what went on between him and Krystle that you'd really rather bust Blaisdel than win him over."

The room was absolutely still for a minute. Even the breeze seemed to be suspended, and the potted palm trees stopped rustling, waiting to see if Blake Carrington was going to explode. But this was his darling daughter, who could do no wrong, and finally he admitted grudgingly, "You just may have had a usable thought."

"As in brilliant?" Fallon asked, grinning widely.

"As in you've made your point. Now go on, get out of here."

She was so pleased with herself that she took the stairs three at a time and bounded into her private sitting room to do a little dance of triumph. And so she missed overhearing an exchange that would have made her evil little heart happier than ever.

There had been nothing for Krystle to do upstairs; two maids were unpacking her things and ironing them before placing them in the too-spacious closets and drawers. She had wandered downstairs to the dining room, where another maid was setting the table.

"Jeanette," she asked, "who will be here for dinner tonight?"

"Just you and Mr. Carrington, ma'am. I'm setting a bit early because there's a dance over in Magordo, and Joseph has given me permission to go."

Krystle smiled. "Of course. But this room is so big and formal, and it'll be beautiful out tonight. I'd like to eat on the terrace."

Suddenly, the young maid was beet red and avoiding her eyes. "Oh, dear, well—you see, ma'am—excuse me but—Joseph prefers all the evening meals to be served in the dining room, you see. He'd have a snit if—"

Her eyes flickered at something, and Krystle turned to look. Joseph was standing at the open door as if he

had just happened to be passing. After a minute, he
went on by.

Jeanette looked terrified. Krystle was a bit shaken
herself. She gentled her voice and said, "It's all right;
we'll eat in here. Everything will be fine. Have a good
time tonight."

Grateful, the maid scampered out. Krystle sat down
on one of the embroidered side chairs, and gazing down
the length of the gleaming mahogany table, began to
understand the need for strategy and planning in a life
as complex as hers was going to be from now on. *Know
your enemies*, she told herself silently. *Suddenly, they
are everywhere.*

Fallon had been watching out the window of her
sitting room, directly above the front door. When Andrew
Laird came out to wait for the car, she called down to
him.

"Wait for me. I'm coming down."

In a minute, she was at his side. "Daddy's really in
trouble this time, isn't he?" she asked quietly.

"You were there. You heard. Or should I say
overheard?"

"What would it take to bail him out?"

"More than your allowance, I'm afraid. What's taking
Michael so long?"

"Can't imagine," she said innocently, although the
chauffeur was watching her for a signal. "How much?"
she asked again.

"Forget it, Fallon," the attorney said impatiently.
"There isn't anything you can do to help."

"You're pretty sure of that, aren't you? You could be
wrong, you know."

Andrew Laird stared at her for a moment, seeming to size her up, although he knew her as well as anyone did. "You really fixed Krystle, didn't you?" he commented, the way one might compliment a rattler for the cleverness of its bite. "Got your father to think about inviting Matthew Blaisdel over here."

"It's the smartest thing for him to do. I don't have to tell you that. If it isn't, he won't do it—"

"It will also make Krystle crazy. And you figure that little by little, chipping away at her, you can drive her out of this house."

He waited for her reply, for once actually looking at her with some interest.

"She's no good for him; she'll drag him down," Fallon muttered.

The dapper, middle-aged attorney sighed. "You know, Fallon, most little girls realize by the age of six that they can't grow up and marry their daddies."

Fallon stepped backward, up the step toward the front door. "Here comes the car," she noted. "*Ciao, consigliere!*" She turned and went inside, slamming the door.

5

"Good evening, Mrs. Carrington. And how has your day been?"

Krystle was brushing her hair hard. She was in her nightgown and robe, seated at the marble table in her dressing room. It was nearly midnight. Blake loosened his tie and took off his jacket as he crossed the white-carpeted bedroom and came through the door toward her. He stooped to kiss her neck.

"Sorry I missed dinner with you, but I was lucky to get out of Washington at all tonight. Terrible fog—hey, what's wrong, love? Bad day?"

She was gritting her teeth, brushing her hair as hard as she could and trying not to catch his eye in one of the mirrors that surrounded them. She was afraid a self-pitying tear might show itself and blow her first chance to talk reasonably and calmly with Blake about the thing that had been weighing on her all day. She didn't trust herself to answer him, and he went on caressing her shoulders, gentling her as he talked.

"What is it—my kids? I know Fallon is spoiled and not easy—and it's frustrating for you—"

"No, it's not that."

"Then what? The party? I guess I should have checked with you before announcing plans for a dinner party.

I'm not used to marriage yet. Well, it hasn't been an easy first week home, has it?"

She turned to him, without the mirrors between them. "It's not the party," she said quietly, in control now. "Joseph will handle it, just like Joseph handles everything. It's—" Krystle's throat was suddenly so dry she had to swallow before she could say it. "Blake, are you actually going to invite Matthew to this house?"

Blake's hands on her shoulders tightened slightly. "Yes. I am," he said.

"Other people are coming—everybody knows about us. Are you that intent on humiliating me in front of other people?"

Blake moved back a step and busied his hands in removing his tie. "I told you, Krystle, having him here is important to me."

"To you. The children are yours. The house is yours. The servants are yours—you spent so much money on me before we were married, why didn't you send me to a school on how to be a guest in your own home? Why didn't you—"

In his incisive, bulldog fashion, Blake fastened onto the one problem that could be dealt with first. "The servants?" he cut in. "What about the servants?"

Krystle shook her head, sorry she had spoken so emotionally. "Never mind; it's nothing," she said.

"Come on," he insisted. "Get it all out."

"Blake, it's okay. Big house, so many people around; I'm new here." She was not going to tattle, to point an accusatory finger at someone else, to get anyone in trouble.

But her husband was insistent, and she saw that he

would not give up. "I want to know about the servants,"
he repeated.

Krystle sighed. "I know it's stupid," she said slowly,
"but—well—it hurts when I can't arrange to have our
dinner served to us on the terrace. When I fold my own
clothes and a maid is offended. The cook has secret
recipes—when I ask about them, he puts me off. Even
the gardener told me he couldn't bring flowers into the
bedroom without an order from you in triplicate."

Blake's stern countenance softened. He touched her
chin with his cupped hand to bring her eyes up to his.
"Why didn't you tell me any of this?" he asked gently.

Her tears about to overflow, she buried her face in his
shirt front. "Because you have really serious problems,
and I don't want to bother you with nonsense. That's
what it is, and I should be able to—" She paused to
reach for a tissue and blow her nose. "To handle it," she
went on, "but I can't. I don't know what to do or what
not to do." She stopped sniffing and looked up at him.
"You want to know the truth, Blake? I'd feel more
comfortable here as one of the staff."

He looked at her for a moment and then reached
onto her dressing table for the house phone. He punched
one number and waited.

"Joseph. Assemble the staff—yes, now!"

Ten minutes later, Blake led Krystle down to the
huge, immaculate kitchen. Brightly lit, the room seemed
cold and oddly bereft without its usual bustle and
enticing smells. The household staff stood in more or
less of a line, all obviously wakened from sleep, all in
robes and slippers. Joseph wore an elegant silk robe
with subtle Chinese embroidery on one cuff.

Blake addressed them, rather like General Patton speaking to the troops.

"Good of you all to come. I thought—that all of you knew my wife." He nodded toward Krystle, who stood dismayed and apprehensive at his side. "Apparently," he went on, "that was an oversight. I'll rectify that by making proper introductions. To begin with, I'd like you to meet Mrs. Blake Carrington. My wife. And the mistress of this house."

Krystle was mortified and embarrassed and ashamed. She touched his arm and murmured, "Blake, please, I don't want to go on with this."

He answered by taking her hand, leading her closer to the row of servants and Joseph, who stood slightly apart. He went down the line, beginning with the young chauffeur.

"This is Michael. He is ambitious. He listens in on conversations which do not concern him. But he drives well. And he might last out the year.

"Gerald pads the grocery bills. Jeanette forgets instructions. Mrs. Gunnerson's several relatives eat well at my expense.

"However, they are all good at their work, and that outweighs their small deficiencies."

"Blake," Krystle pleaded, "please stop this."

"My wife is concerned for you," Blake announced to the servants. "Are any of you uncomfortable?" They were silent. "Good," he said, "then I'll go on. Leon, how long have you been with me?" he asked an elderly man, whose weather-beaten face had not been shaved before retiring and who was visibly trembling.

"Ten years, sir," the old man answered shyly.

"Working my gardens"—Blake nodded—"the man in

charge of all the other labor we bring in to help you."

"Yes," the gardener nodded.

"Did you recently have a conversation with my wife about flowers?"

"Uh—I think so—yes," Leon answered nervously.

"And did she ask you during the course of that conversation to place some flowers in our bedroom?"

"That's right—she did—"

"And did you tell her that I didn't want flowers in my bedroom?"

The old man was answering eagerly now. "Yes, sir. You always said—"

Blake cut in sharply. "Mrs. Carrington loves flowers in her room. I do not. But I'll get used to that. What I will not get used to is rudeness. Pack your bags. I want you out of here in the morning." He turned to the others. "The rest of you will understand that what I have tried to convey is that you are all dispensable to me. My wife is not. Good night."

He pivoted on his heel and strode out of the kitchen, leaving Krystle, miserable and barely able to hold back her tears, facing the hostile group of servants. She turned and rushed from the room.

He was waiting for her on the stairs. "How could you do that?" She gasped. "Blake, I didn't want that man fired. That's the last thing I—"

He put his arm around her and led her slowly up the stairs.

"Tomorrow morning," he said, "Joseph will come to me and say that Leon has apologized, that he would like his job back. And I will give him his job back. And the others will all say, 'Mr. Carrington is a hard man, but a fair man.' Krystle, darling, I can't expect you to

know all of this right away. About how to run this
house, about why certain guests must be asked to
dinner—yes, that's part of it, too. But I'll teach you,
and you'll learn. It's your house, Krystle, and more
than anything in the world, I want you to make it your
home. Now let's go to bed."

And she knew he was right. It was going to be
damned hard, but she could do it—all of it, one step at
a time. Starting with facing Matthew Blaisdel across her
own dinner table. And even, maybe, learning to make a
friend out of her unhappy stepdaughter. Fallon was a
different kind of problem, but with her husband's arms
enfolding her, Krystle fell asleep.

Fallon's biggest problem right now was Cecil Colby.
She wanted him. Not just to seduce him, but to marry,
because he was the most magnetically attractive man
she had ever known. A few years older than her father,
he had never married, making him, of course, an
irresistible challenge to every woman who ever met
him. Fallon's instinctive rise to any challenge was
heightened by the fact that her father had been trying
to catch up to and outdistance Cecil Colby since long
before she was born. Even as a young wildcatter, Blake
Carrington had set his sights on Colby as the man to
beat. But the older man had always been there first—
the best leases, the richest strikes, the sharpest deals,
the luckiest gambles.

Fallon had cut her teeth on her daddy's rivalry with
Cecil Colby and their mutual admiration; she had watched
the two giants locking horns like proud stags in the
wild, and she had been present when they dined
together as friends. All her life, Fallon had been in-

trigued by the man who could stay ahead of her father
in the all-important games of wealth and power.

She was accustomed to manipulating men, especially
the soft-eyed boys who claimed to love her and would
do absolutely anything she wanted them to. They bored
her to tears. The appeal of Cecil Colby was irresistible.
Ever since the night of her father's wedding when they
had gone off together in the car, Fallon had been
scheming to get alone with Cecil Colby again.

And one evening she had her chance. Guests at the
same dinner party, Fallon Carrington and Cecil Colby
found themselves, by her finagling, leaving the dining
room side by side. The other guests retired to the
drawing room for brandy; Fallon, her green eyes impishly
daring, suggested a walk out on the grounds and Colby,
amused and obviously, she thought, attracted, agreed.
They slipped out one of the French doors that fronted
the dining-room terrace and were soon walking along
the sheltered paths of their host's formal garden. Fallon
was wearing lime-green chiffon, cut to show off her tiny
waist and baring her shoulders and throat. She hadn't
bothered with a wrap and didn't feel the need for one.

"I heard something delicious about you in the pow-
der room just before dinner," she teased.

"Something scandalous, no doubt." Colby laughed
easily.

Fallon shook her long dark curls. "*Au contraire*," she
answered. "The word was that Fitzie Randolph's wife
came on to you last week and you told her to get lost.
She's not that unsexy, is she?"

"*Au contraire*," Colby answered, grinning. "She's
very sexy." He took her arm and tucked it through his
as they walked. He was almost as tall as her father and

walked with the same purposeful stride. In the moonlight, she found his profile heartbreakingly handsome. She matched her steps to his and thought she could feel his heart beating next to her arm as he held it.

He was talking a bit like the elder statesman, though, the way her father did sometimes when he had a lesson to impart. "Fallon," Colby was saying, "I've been called an unprincipled conglomerateur, many times. And worse. But I do have certain principles, believe it or not. And one of them has to do with the sanctity of marriage. People being faithful to their vows and old-fashioned stuff like that. I do not take up with ladies who are married to other men."

"Good," she commented. "That makes me available!"

He stopped walking and looked down into her eager, pert, and very appealing, moonlit face. And then he kissed her, not passionately but not like an uncle, either. She melted, ready to make love then and there, but when their lips separated, he held her a little apart. Fallon opened her eyes to see that somehow a serious note had crept in between them, and he had something to say. She reached up to touch her finger tip against his cheek, but he caught her hand and held it.

"If we were going to proceed with this," he said, "I'd whisk you off somewhere, believe me. Somewhere romantic and certainly more private. But you and I have business to talk about, don't we, Fallon? Out in the open."

"Do we?" She sighed.

"Your father's in deep trouble. You want me to help him."

She pulled away from him. His hands dropped to his sides. "I didn't say that," she answered cautiously.

"Is it true or not?"

She countered with her own question. "Can you help him?"

"Yes."

There was a little wooden bench carved out of a huge oak tree, part of the tree and yet a welcoming seat for anyone who wished to sit and be contemplative in the middle of the serene garden. Fallon walked away from Colby the few steps to the oak and sat down. He followed and stood looking down at her. "I want you to marry Jeff," he said calmly.

Her eyes flashed. "I'd rather marry you," she told him.

Colby smiled. "That's very sweet," he said, "but you and I have other reasons for what we do beyond what we want for ourselves."

"I wouldn't be any good for Jeff," she told him honestly.

"He adores you. I want him to settle down with someone smart, smarter than he is, even brilliant. That's you, Fallon. If he became your family, you could help him. Not that he's stupid, but with your brains behind him—"

"And in exchange you'd bail out my father."

"Exactly. You know, Jeff's not such a bad catch. He's plenty bright, good-looking, caring. And heir apparent to Colbyco—a sort of Colorado version of the Prince of Wales."

Fallon was too restless to sit there like a passive Victorian maiden waiting to hear what some man had decided her fate was to be. She stood up and started to walk again. Cecil Colby strode easily at her side. They didn't touch. Finally, she spoke.

"Cecil, when I marry, what I want is to lie beside a man who excites me, to look forward all day, every day, to the nights—isn't that important? You excite me, Cecil. Jeff doesn't."

Colby smiled a bit ruefully. "Listen to me, my dear," he said. "Passion dies. Power remains. There aren't that many young men in this world who'll be as powerful as Jeff Colby. If he has someone to direct him, direct his drive. It's there. He needs guidance, stirring up. 'Stimulation'—that's the word. Something I obviously haven't been able to provide. But with you—the two of you could fly as high as you wanted to, no limits. That's power—that's passion, too; only you don't know it yet. A more lasting kind, believe me."

She didn't answer. She thought her heart might be breaking. But she was also thinking about his offer to pull Blake out of his present difficulties. Hadn't she heard Andrew say that he might be close to bankruptcy— unthinkable—and yet the lawyer had said it, and Blake was really worried this time. And here was the only other man in the state, or in the country, maybe, big enough and rich enough and interested enough to pull him out.

"Fallon," Colby was saying, "I know the most important thing in the world to you is Blake. And you and I both know that I'm the one who can help him most. Say the word and—"

"How can you do it, and how soon?" she interrupted coldly.

"Immediately. And in a way that he'll never find out where it came from. You have my word on that."

She turned to face him. "And what if I were to

change my mind?" she taunted. "Didn't keep my end of the bargain? What would you do then?"

Colby smiled. "Let's just say that at my age getting even is as sweet as making love."

Fallon knew he was not threatening idly. This was a man who would use his power in whatever ruthless way suited him and his own interests best. Someday she would have that kind of power, too. She hoped, fleetingly, that Cecil Colby would still be around when she came into her own.

They were nearing the house where their absence would surely have been noticed by now. Lights blazed from all the windows. Cecil stopped walking just before they reached the bright arc of light that fell over the steps leading up to the terrace. He turned to her.

"What do you say, Fallon? Do we have a deal?" he asked.

Fallon waited for a full minute, then two, before holding out her right hand to shake on it.

She told no one of her decision, of the deal—not even Jeff. He could hang around, proposing, for a while. He wouldn't go anywhere, and she wasn't in any hurry to tie the knot. Impulsively, Fallon flew off to Europe for a couple of weeks just "for the hell of it." When she came home, she saw a new, huge emerald solitaire on a gold chain around Krystle's neck. That was when Fallon began to suspect that Cecil Colby had already kept his part of the bargain.

"That's new," she commented when Krystle came downstairs dressed to go out. She wore the deep-faceted green gem on its chain over a soft, simply cut white silk dress that floated down to the floor, only

grazing her slim curves here and there as it went. Even
Fallon had to admit, but only to herself, that Krystle
was a knockout-looking lady. But it was the gem that
interested her. Her stepmother seemed embarrassed,
just a smidgeon, in the heat of Fallon's pointed stare.

"Like it?" her father asked cheerfully. "Goes with
Krystle's eyes, doesn't it?"

"You must be back in the chips," Fallon commented.

"Either that or it's million-dollar spit-in-the-ocean
time." Blake laughed, not letting her in on anything.
Fallon was a tiny bit gratified to see Krystle's bewildered look—at least she knew exactly what her father
was saying. If you were in trouble, that was the time to
bluff. "Where's your brother tonight?" her father asked,
changing the subject as if she were a kid or something.

Fallon shrugged. "Am I my brother's keeper?" she
asked, flipping the pages of her magazine.

"Ever since he started working for Matthew Blaisdel,
he's been avoiding me," Blake commented. "As if I
would be angry about his getting an honest job—"

"He goes to work at six in the morning, Dad. He's
probably sleeping by now. It's almost nine o'clock."
Fallon yawned elaborately and stretched her arms. "I
don't imagine he's thinking about you one way or the
other," she said, stealing a glance at her father to see if
he was properly annoyed.

It wasn't that she was covering for Steven, but she
had a hunch her brother really wouldn't want Blake to
know that he was, at this very moment, in a hotel room
in downtown Denver with his ex-roommate and lover,
Ted Milton. Ted had phoned in late afternoon, and
Fallon had taken the call. On his way to San Francisco,
Ted had stopped over in Denver, staying at the Brown

Palace Hotel, and wondered if Steven would spend the evening with him. Fallon, listening to Ted's voice on the phone and the pain behind it, suddenly understood. When Steven had come home from work in his dirty overalls and denim shirt, she had given him Ted's message.

Steven had been startled and visibly upset, but he had called Ted and gone to him. Fallon would protect her brother any way she could. It was her second greatest loyalty, after that which she felt for her father. But Blake Carrington didn't seem to need her—at least not right now, while the bloom was still on his new marriage—and would never know the sacrifice she had made for him. Feeling a bit sorry for herself, a bit like a tribal virgin bartered for a sack of grain, Fallon threw down the magazine, and with a quick glimpse in the mirror over the hall table, wandered out to the garage. But Michael was driving her father and Krystle. Peevishly, she phoned Jeff and ordered him to take her out for a long, fast drive.

In the bar of the Brown Palace Hotel, Steven and Ted were having their reunion. From their seat in a dark corner, they noticed a party of two couples celebrating an anniversary a few tables away. One of the men in that group was a coworker of Steven's. Big Ed kept eying the two young men as they talked quietly but intensely.

"You can't really mean to stay here forever," Ted said, half joking and half pleading.

"I don't know. Yes, maybe. I want to make something of my life, and this is where my roots are."

"Oh, come on, Steven. You hate your father. Now you're living in the same house with him. I just don't understand why. Why you left me—"

"Hey, Ted, don't. Please don't. It wasn't you I left, it was New York and that whole scene—I just wanted to grow up, I guess. Stop playing party boy and take on some responsibility. I'm sorry if you can't understand that."

"I do. I do, Steven. Only—I miss you so much. The apartment is so empty, and nobody to argue with about who does the dishes or takes out the garbage."

"You could get another roommate."

"That's cruel, Steven. You know how much I—care for you. Love you."

Steven said something in a tone so low that Ted had to lean his head very close to hear. "What?"

Steven looked up, and there were tears in his eyes. He whispered, "I said I love you, too, but it's all over."

Ted reached out his arm around Steven's shoulders. Their eyes met and held for a moment, and then they both tried to smile and lifted their glasses in a silent, private toast.

Only it was not so private as they thought.

Steven had said nothing to anyone about his working day on the Lankershim-Blaisdel rig. But Matthew Blaisdel saw at least part of the harassment and butt kicking that were part of Steven's work load every hour on the job. There was nothing he could do to make it easier on the kid even if he had wanted to. But Steven had learned to use his wits and humor for survival, and exchanges like this had started to win over even the hardest hard hats on the rig:

"You know what you got there, kid? That there's a blister."

Playing along, Steven answered, "Really?"

"You know what that comes from?" someone asked in a mockingly helpful tone.

"You tell me."

"Squeezing your polo mallet too tight," the wit replied to the guffaws of the other workers.

"You wanna watch that stuff," Big Ed chimed in.

"No, you watch it, Ed," Steven answered evenly. The laughs stopped as the men edged in to listen, not sure what to expect. Big Ed had a trigger temper. He waited, glowering. "You be careful," Steven wound up, "or I'll hit you in the fist with my nose and bleed all over you."

The riggers broke out laughing, and Big Ed had to laugh, too, but he always got the last word. "Hey, Bobby," he would shout, "bring some of that diaper-rash ointment over here!"

Every time they broke for coffee or lunch or had to stand around waiting for a pipe to be tested or wiring to be done, the game would begin again. But, Matthew was gratified to observe, Steven Carrington was earning the men's respect on his own, the hard way. Calloused and sunburned and muscle-bound, he worked as hard as any man on the crew.

Matthew had his doubts about Blake Carrington, though. Lots of doubts. What in the hell was he doing, inviting them to dinner? Crusty old Walter, who might not even bother to shave before showing up at the mansion, and himself and Claudia—what was that all about? He was positive it couldn't have been Krystle's idea. It would be just as uncomfortable for her as it would for him. The two of them, who once loved each other so much that you could almost see the electricity in the air when they were in the same room—to sit at dinner between their two spouses and make polite conversation? It was ludicrous, impossible.

And yet here he was, tying his black tie, watching Claudia put on a long dress and the good opal earrings he had bought her for their tenth anniversary. Claudia was pleased and a little bit excited about going to the Carringtons for dinner.

He turned to her. "You look nice," he said.

"Thank you," she answered.

He went to her and put his hands on her shoulders. He felt her recoil slightly from his touch.

"You don't want me to touch you," he said.

He stood there, not knowing what to do. He tried again. He smiled. "Later, tonight, when we come home. . . ."

She caught his hand and pressed it to her cheek, only for a moment, and then let go. "Oh, I hope so," she said.

"I wish we didn't have to go at all," Matthew exclaimed suddenly. "Why did I let myself get roped into this, anyway?"

"Well," Claudia answered. "Walter said you ought to go and find out what Blake is up to, and I wanted to meet Mrs. Carrington, and—"

"Okay, okay. Come on, then. I suppose we'd better get going. I'll go say good night to Lindsay."

Claudia nodded and smiled until he left the room, and then she sat there wondering why she felt like crying.

The dinner party was elegant, even regal. The table was set for fourteen, with long, even lines of shining crystal, gleaming china, and heavy silver on ivory damask.

Instead of the traditional centerpieces, small bouquets of fresh flowers sat at each place setting in tiny cut-glass bowls. Krystle and Blake faced each other from opposite ends of the long table and kept the conversation animated, cheerful, and bright. Matthew found himself seated at Blake's end of the table, with the wife of one of Denver-Carrington's vice presidents between them. Claudia was opposite him, apparently getting along very well with Steven Carrington. Matthew hadn't seen his wife so animated in a very long time, and he was glad for her. She was really having a good time, and maybe things would work out later. He tried to keep his glance from Krystle's end of the table.

She was incredibly lovely tonight, wearing a pale-yellow dress that caught the colors in her hair exactly. The diamonds in her ears put all the other jewels of all the other women in the room to shame; only Krystle's eyes, Matthew thought, could live up to those diamonds and outshine them, too. He forced himself to listen to Mrs. Harrison's long story about the problems she was having with her gardener.

At last, dinner was over, and they moved into the living room for brandy. Matthew wondered if Blake might seek him out, to talk with him or Walter and reveal the real reason for this invitation. But their host was involved in what looked like serious talk with Cecil Colby. Matthew's eyes involuntarily sought out Krystle. She was alone for the moment, standing near the open doors to the terrace. He moved toward her.

"Too bad you had to cut your honeymoon short because of a little revolution overseas," Cecil Colby was saying to his host.

"A minor setback, Cecil," Blake Carrington scoffed.

Colby shook his head. "Blake, Blake—you tell the other fellas in the room that, maybe they'll believe you. But you and I, we go back to the ice age. And I know you've got a fortune locked up over there."

"True, Cecil," Blake answered smoothly, easily. "One fortune. But only one."

Cecil played at being chagrined. "Now I am embarrassed," he said. "I came running over, waving my checkbook like a life preserver, and I find you floating happily in the sun. Forgive me."

He gave Blake an affectionate pat on the arm, sipped at his brandy, and started to move away toward a cluster of people who were admiring a Matisse nearby. But Blake moved to block his way.

"On the other hand," Blake said, smiling, "suppose— just suppose—I could use a bit of tiding over. What do you figure it would cost me?"

"Not much," Colby assured him. "Say"—Blake followed his glance across the room to Walter Lankershim, who, with brandy in one hand and cigar in the other, was regaling two other guests with some story or other—"a piece of the Lankershim-Blaisdel leases?"

Blake's face clouded slightly. "I may be in a little trouble, Cecil," he said, "but I won't be robbed at gunpoint. Not even by my best friend."

Now it was his turn to start to move away and Colby's to stop him.

"Hey—Blake. You can't blame a fellow for trying, can you?"

Blake looked at him, and the cloud lifted. "Hell, I would have done the same thing myself," he said, enjoying the moment.

"Suppose I said it wouldn't cost you anything," Colby went on.

"I wouldn't trust it." Blake laughed easily.

"Maybe we'll just call it a good-faith loan," Colby said, "from one prospective in-law to another."

Blake, surprised, followed Colby's glance toward the corner where Fallon and Jeff sat talking animatedly, probably arguing. "Cecil, do you know something I don't know?" he asked.

Colby laughed. "Meet me at the Petroleum Club Monday for lunch. We'll work out the details."

Now he did move off to admire the painting. Blake looked around the room for Krystle, but she had stepped outside apparently, and his arm was taken by a garrulous Mrs. Harrison, who wanted to know all about how he liked married life.

And outside, on the terrace, Krystle talked with Matthew Blaisdel. They stood looking out at the stretch of garden and orchard that swept down past the lawn on this side of the house.

"Nice little place you've got here," Matthew said.

"It's small, but it's home," she joked.

"I expect, come Saturday morning, Blake gets out there with his lawnmower and his weed puller—"

Krystle laughed. "You get a picture of that and we'll sell it to *People* magazine."

He turned to lean against the stone railing and look at her in the soft lamplight from the windows. "You've got a good life, Krystle," he said sincerely. "I'm really glad for you."

Krystle nodded, avoiding his eyes. "I like your wife," she said.

"Yes, I figured you would if you ever got to meet her. She's a good person, Claudia. A very good person—"

"Yes."

"She deserves more than I can give her."

"If you came in with Blake, you could be very rich," Krystle said. "He wants you and Walter to turn the leases over to him entirely, you know. It would be part of Denver-Carrington then, and that means big time, big money."

Matthew turned away and gazed out past the trees to the dark sky. "Is this why you invited me to dinner?" he asked coolly.

Krystle touched his arm to turn him back toward her. "Blake is set up to help you develop that property, Matthew. He can make you a very wealthy man—"

Matthew's voice was icy steel when he cut in on her pleading. "So that's what he's got you doing for him. Do you know what that work is called, Krystle? I can't believe it; you're actually trying to buy me for him. Is it also your job to supply women for out-of-town executives and—"

She gasped, and he choked back the rest of the hurtful words. "I didn't realize you hated me so," she said finally.

Matthew's emotional turmoil was so strong that his next words came spilling out of their own volition, and he was powerless to stop them. "Hate you? I don't hate you, Krystle. I love you."

The earth stopped spinning for a long moment, everything suspended in time, and all the sounds of the dinner party faded into the distance. When Krystle recovered her senses, Matthew was mumbling an apology and moving away from her. She put out her hand to stop him.

"Matthew, look at me," she managed to say.

When he did, he said what he felt. "I guess I can't help it, Krystle. I guess I'll always love you."

For a long, empty moment, they both struggled with the meaning of this thing that had finally come out. But for Krystle there was an additional emotion, something approaching betrayal.

"But when you came back, when we met, just before I got married, you said—" She was having trouble getting the words out. "You said—you didn't care for me anymore."

"I did what I thought was best for you—for both of us—at the time," Matthew answered miserably.

"Am I supposed to be grateful to you for that?" she whispered. "Who the hell gave you the right to make that judgment for me? I am not a child, Matthew. I am a grown woman! I have the right to make decisions about my own life!"

"I understand that, Krystle. I was only trying to—"

"No! You don't understand. I would have settled for a small piece of something good, Matthew—"

Someone opened the door from the living room just then, and two people sauntered out into the cool evening air. Krystle brushed past them, hurrying into the house. "Will you excuse me, please," she managed to say.

In the garden below the terrace, where she had gone for a toke of grass and found herself listening to her stepmother and Matthew Blaisdel, Fallon Carrington stretched herself and got up to go back inside. Maybe things weren't going to be as dull as she had thought.

6

Matthew was more than usually silent on the drive home from the Carrington dinner party. In contrast, Claudia was bubbling. It had been a wonderful evening for her. She liked the new Mrs. Carrington, and she had enjoyed talking to everyone, especially young Steven. On the drive home, she tried to convey some of her excitement to her husband.

"Did you get a chance to talk to Blake?" she asked.

"Yes."

"Well? Did you find out why he wanted you and Walter to come tonight?"

"Never was a mystery, Claudia. I knew from the beginning—he wants our leases. He even got his wife to push for it."

"Well, no need to be so glum, honey. You didn't give it to him, did you?"

"Of course not."

They drove in silence for a while.

"Walter seemed to be enjoying himself," Claudia ventured.

"I guess so."

More silence.

"You must be tired," Claudia said as they were

turning into their own street. She didn't know it, but she sighed.

"Yes I am, bone tired," Matthew agreed. He pulled to a stop in their driveway and turned off the motor.

"Well, I had a good time," Claudia said, getting out of the car. But he slammed the door on his side of the car and didn't hear her.

He's got a lot on his mind, and he's tired, she thought to herself, lying awake next to him later. *Poor Matthew.* She smiled to herself in the dark. That was a switch—she was feeling sorry for someone else instead of poor Claudia. Drifting slowly toward sleep, she thought about the evening. Steven Carrington had made her feel—well, pretty and young and, yes, desirable. He was a warm, straightforward, and handsome boy.

At the dinner table, he had made her laugh. "That sandwich you gave me out on the rig that day was exactly the right combination of ingredients that I needed. Salami on white bread. A little proletarian, but it gave me the strength to take on the hordes of Genghis Khan."

"What on earth are you talking about? I remember the sandwich, but then what happened?" she asked, intrigued.

"That was the day I got the job on your husband's crew," he said. "But first I had to fight a guy. Really. Never could have done it without the salami on white."

"Did you win?"

"No. I lost the fight. But I got the job."

Claudia laughed. "I should have put the salami on rye," she said. "Then you might have had a better chance."

"Ah, but if I'd won the fight, I probably wouldn't have gotten the job," he said. "That's the way the world is out there, totally nuts."

"I guess so," she answered cheerfully.

"Well, you tell me," Steven went on, "are all the lunatics locked up? Or are most of them walking around pretending to be politicians and captains of industry?"

Claudia took a sip of her wine before answering. "Am I supposed to be some kind of expert?" she asked carefully.

"You've been in a mental hospital, haven't you?"

"Yes."

"Hey, I'm sorry. I guess that was really crude of me. If you're sensitive about it, we don't have to—"

"It's not that," she said quickly.

"Then what is it?"

She looked at his open, intelligent, friendly face. "I'm not sure," she said slowly. "Most people aren't quite as direct as you are. But actually it's kind of refreshing. I'm getting a little tired of being treated as if I had a social disease. People lowering their voices and talking about the weather because they don't want to upset the Madwoman."

"Some of the greatest people in history have done time on the flip side," Steven said cheerfully. "Nijinsky. Peter the Great. Dostoevski. Virginia Woolf. You're in pretty good company."

Claudia laughed. "I'll remember that when things get—gloomy."

Steven looked genuinely concerned. "Hey, things shouldn't ever get gloomy for you," he said, and she could have sworn he blushed. "You're too pretty," he finished, and then seemed relieved when their hostess asked him a question that brought them into the main-stream of general conversation.

But later Steven had asked her to come into the library with him, and there he had given her a small leather-bound book of Emily Dickinson's poems.

"Emily Dickinson was special," he told her earnestly, "and I think you are, too. Please, I want you to have this."

Lying beside her sleeping husband, Claudia thought about Steven Carrington. He was seven or eight years younger than she was. But he had made her feel attractive and interesting—even beautiful. After a while, she got up, as she often did, but instead of taking a pill, she took the little leather-bound book from her evening bag and went downstairs to read poetry until she grew sleepy.

The morning after the dinner party, Krystle woke to find Blake already gone and the sun pouring into her bedroom like a benign rebuke. She jumped out of bed and went to the window, letting the hot sun flood over her as if to burn away guilt and loss and pain and regret. The garden below was a lovely sprawl of colors meticulously planned to seem casual, blending like the rainbow colors in gradual stages from pale pinks to deep purples. Beyond lay the soft grass of the wide lawn and the sparkling blue of the pool.

Krystle sat down at her desk to make a phone call, then another and another. She should have realized before embarrassing her friends that no one could lunch with her. There just wasn't time on a one-hour break to drive up here, eat, and get back to the office, much less have a real old-fashioned talk or a swim in the pool.

She breakfasted alone by the shimmering cool water, had a brisk swim, climbed out, dried her hair, and picked up a novel she had found in the library. She was emerging from another swim break when she looked up to see Joseph coming toward her. She watched the officious, unsmiling major-domo as he stepped carefully around the puddles she had kicked up alongside the blue marble edge. As she ascended the pool ladder, he picked up her terry-cloth robe and held it for her with every expectation that she would obediently slip into it.

It seemed to her that he held off speaking until just a sliver this side of rudeness. She waited, poised halfway up the ladder, still half in the water and thinking she might just want to slide back under the cool blue surface and float underwater until this unpleasant man bugged out of her life. But she waited, looking at him expectantly, and finally he had to speak first.

"Excuse me, Mrs. Carrington, but Mr. Beaumont is here to see you," he said with something like impatience just under the surface politeness.

She had no idea what this was about. "Mr. Beaumont?"

Joseph stood there holding her robe and still managing to look superior. "Yes, ma'am. Mr. James Beaumont, the couturier. He's just arrived from New York. He has an appointment to see you—you do know about it?"

It was pretty obvious that she didn't, but she was damned if she'd give him the satisfaction of admitting her ignorance. "Yes, of course," she said, climbing out of the pool. She slid her arm into the robe, trying not to get any water on him. "Will you tell Mr. Beaumont I'll only be a few moments, Joseph, please," she said.

"I've already done that," Joseph said. He let go of the

robe as though to avoid contagion and started back toward the house.

Toweling her hair furiously, Krystle realized that it was now or never, and she called after him. "Joseph, I wonder if you and I could find a moment to talk. There are some things I'd like to—" But he was gone.

She had never heard of Mr. James Beaumont, but he could wait. Krystle forced herself to breathe slowly and deeply on her way to the house, and by the time she reached the household office corridor, she was quite calm. She knocked on Joseph's door and went inside.

He was sitting at his desk and didn't bother to stand when she came in.

She spoke quietly, as she always did, but her words belied the softness of her voice. "I'll make this short, Joseph. I don't like rudeness, not from anyone, and I don't plan to go on tolerating it. Yes, I am intimidated by this house, but I had hoped you would help me to make it my home. Mr. Carrington told you that I am here to stay, and I think you'd better believe it. Can we have a truce, Joseph, you and I?" She wondered if she should hold out her hand but settled for a friendly smile across his neat desk.

Now he did stand. "I'm afraid I don't know what you are referring to," he said coolly.

Krystle felt her knees tremble. She hoped her face didn't give her away. "I'll bet if you think about it, it will come to you," she said shortly. "And now I mustn't keep Mr. Beaumont waiting."

She felt immeasurably better and almost laughed out loud as she ran up the stairs two at a time, her terry-cloth robe flying behind her. She dressed quickly in well-pressed blue denim slacks and a bright silk shirt and came back down the stairs more sedately.

In the library, a man whose name was familiar to the readers of international fashion magazines waited for her. He was impeccably groomed and fit into this elegant room with ease. Krystle's hair was still damp from swimming, and she was still perplexed about his visit.

He smiled and introduced himself. Then he opened a large sketchbook and began to show her drawing after drawing of dresses, suits, and gowns. Krystle just sat there, listening and looking, her fidgets increasing each time his manicured fingers flipped a page.

"Of course these are just preliminary sketches based on some notions of Mr. Carrington's," Beaumont was saying, "and once we've had a chance to talk, I'll have a better idea of how your taste runs. Then we can have a dressmaker's form built to your measurements, and while you and I are picking out fabrics—"

She couldn't keep silent another instant. "Excuse me, Mr. Beaumont," she cut in, "but how much do you suppose all of this is going to cost?"

He was startled. The question was so unexpected that he obviously wasn't even sure he had heard it correctly.

"I—I beg your pardon."

"The clothes," Krystle said. "All the stuff you're talking about. How much will it cost?"

The couturier glanced around, partly out of embarrassment, partly in the unlikely hope that someone would magically intercede and deliver him from having to answer Mrs. Carrington's gauche and unprecedented question. But no one appeared, and she waited impatiently for him to say something.

"Actually," he said uncomfortably, "that's something that's usually discussed between—uh—Mr. Carrington and myself."

Krystle was no more comfortable than he was, but she pressed on. "I understand," she said, "but I would still like to know. How much?"

The wretched man shuffled through his sketches, stalling. "Well, I'd have to give that a little thought. Perhaps if you could wait unti—"

"Tell her, Mr. B."

Krystle and Beaumont both turned around to see Fallon, who had been doing her usual stint of eavesdropping, leaning against the open door with her arms folded across her chest. She looked amused. "Go ahead, tell her how much the clothes are going to cost. It's all right."

Still reluctant, he gave in. "Your wardrobe," he said, avoiding Krystle's eyes, "for the season—dresses, gowns, accessories—should run somewhere between seventy-five and a hundred." He looked up at her and added quickly, "Thousand."

She tried not to look as shocked as she felt. Before she had a chance to recover, Beaumont added another afterthought. "That's not including furs," he said.

Outflanked by the designer's reluctance and her stepdaughter's obvious delight, Krystle forced herself to press on.

"Are you sure Mr. Carrington wanted me to order all this? I mean, I have to tell you the truth. He never said a word to me about it." She felt herself blushing.

Before Beaumont could respond, Fallon interceded brightly. "Daddy's such a planner. Does the same thing to me all the time. Just sneaks in while I'm asleep and leaves a note in my pillow saying—"

But, cutting Fallon off, Krystle turned to Beaumont and said, "Please excuse me, Mr. Beaumont, but I just can't—I mean, I'll have to have a word with Mr. Carrington before I can—" Unable to finish, she turned away from the incredulous man and hurried past Fallon out of the room.

Fallon told Beaumont to relax, fix himself a drink, and wait. Then she hurried upstairs after Krystle, following her into the open door of the master bedroom without waiting for an invitation.

Krystle was standing at the night table near her bed, reading a note she had just found there.

"See, was I wrong?" Fallon asked cheerily. "He left you a note."

But Krystle remained unconvinced. "I know that Blake is trying to do something nice for me, but—well, right now, with all his financial problems, this is no time to—" Instead of finishing the sentence, she went to the dressing room and opened one of the mirrored doors. "I've got a closetful of beautiful things he's bought me already," she finished limply. Oh, how she wished her stepdaughter would understand!

Fallon's answer dissuaded Krystle of any such notion. "Those are things Blake Carrington bought for his girl friend," she said coldly. "You're his wife now."

Stung, Krystle took on a hard edge of her own. "I'm sorry, Fallon," she said, "but this is not your concern. This is something that your father and I will have to discuss."

Fallon looked at her with ill-concealed contempt. Then she smiled, that incredible sunny grin of hers that belied her true disposition. "You know, Krystle," she said with a shrug, "you haven't exactly won over everybody in this house."

Krystle turned away. "I'm beginning to believe that," she answered wearily.

"If somebody tries to help you out—well, I should think you'd take the time to listen."

With that, Fallon turned and started out of the room.

Terribly unsure of herself, scared and alone, Krystle turned around. "Fallon—Fallon, I'm listening."

Fallon turned. "You've got some things to learn about how rich people function, particularly in times of crisis."

"And you're going to teach me?"

"Yes. Enough to keep you from making a total fool of yourself, for starters."

"Oh, Fallon, I wish I could trust you. I wish we could be friends, but somehow I just wonder why you're being so helpful all of a sudden. I certainly haven't won you over—"

"That's right, you haven't. But if you embarrass yourself, you embarrass my father. And I won't let that happen. Sit down, Krystle."

Krystle found herself sinking into one of the needle-pointed wing chairs that flanked the little round table near the north windows. Fallon sat in the other and went on with her lecture.

"The rich are different, Krystle—don't make any mistake about that. The poor cut back in hard times; that's why they stay poor. But the rich know that's the time to spend. Important people watch us and judge. They like to support winners, and they turn away from

losers like the sun sinks in the west. They judge
whether Blake Carrington's table is brilliantly set, whether his servants continue to respect him, and how well
his wife and daughter are dressed. And from those
things, they know the state of his mind—and the strength
of his resolve. Can you understand that?"

Krystle understood enough to say simply, "What shall
I do?"

"Call Joseph up here and tell him to take the clothes
you've already worn downstairs and divide them among
the servants. Then go and see James Beaumont. He's
still waiting for you downstairs. Don't apologize to him,
by the way."

Krystle thought about the advice. Then she held out
her hand to her stepdaughter, across the Pierre Deux
fabric that covered the table between them. "Thank
you, Fallon."

But Fallon shook her head. "It's not a gift," she said
haughtily, ignoring Krystle's hand. "I'll tell you something
else that might be helpful while we're in such a confidential mood. Rich people have to watch out for scandals."

"I don't understand?"

"Oh," Fallon said breezily, getting up from the chair
and heading for the door again, "it's just that I went to a
party the other night, and while I was having a breath
of air out near the terrace, I heard this couple talking.
She admitted she'd rather have been his mistress than
the wife of the man she's just married. If that got out,
whew! *Quel scandale!*" With that, she sauntered out of
the room, leaving Krystle to fight back her tears alone.

Let her think he's still in trouble, she decided as she
went down the winding stairs. She could have told
Krystle—after the lecture, of course—that Blake's finan-

cial crisis had been resolved. It would have been fun to
see Krystle's face as it dawned on her that Blake
confided in his daughter and not in his wife. But that
was kid stuff. There were more satisfying games to play;
and anyway, Fallon would never, never discuss family
business with an outsider.

She missed Steven. Her brother was the only person
in the world she could really talk to honestly. Steven
didn't make judgments or shrug her off because she was
only a girl. But Steven was living out at the rig now,
sharing the life of the other workers and proving that he
could make it on his own, without Blake's help.

Life in the bunkhouse was mostly poker, guitar picking,
and reading magazines. Steven found it oddly satisfying,
a kind of hiatus in his life when no more was expected
of him than of the next man. He worked hard and came
back physically exhausted every night and was getting
along just fine without thinking about the future—or
the past.

The poker game was just winding down. Walter,
Matthew, and three of the riggers were playing nickel-
dime draw. Steven was reading on his bunk when Big
Ed came in, drunk but on his feet.

"Evening! I'm back!" he called to no one in particular.

Walter looked up from the pot he had just scooped in
with a straight flush. "We see you," he said loudly, "and
we smell you. Cheapest bourbon in town, he'll find it,"
he confided to the others.

Big Ed lurched toward Steven, then stopped. He
turned back to the poker table. "How's it been going?"
he asked in drunken mock seriousness. "All you guys
safe?"

Annoyed at having his concentration distracted, Walter called over his shoulder, "Ed, get under a cold shower and hit the sack!"

"What? And take my chances when the lights go out? I'll tell you this, Lankersheim—I ain't sleeping in the same room with him." He pointed unsteadily toward Steven, who could no longer pretend to be absorbed in his book. He felt himself flush darkly.

"Shut up, Ed," Matthew said tersely. "Walter told you to—"

"Take a shower. Not with him around, no, sir!" Reeling, he fell against one of the bunks but recovered his balance and started to mince on tiptoe toward Steven. In an instant, Matthew was up and grappling with him. Big Ed's fighting instincts came up from the floor, and a hard, accurate punch landed on Matthew Blaisdel's jaw. The two went at it hard and silent except for the involuntary grunts and the sound of knuckles hitting bone. It was over in a few moments, with Big Ed laid out cold on the floor.

Steven stood near his bunk, apart from the others, who had gathered around to watch the fight. Matthew, bruised and bloodied, came over to him, taking his arm to lead him outside under the still, clear desert sky.

"Thanks," Steven said. "But I would have taken him on—"

Matthew grunted because it hurt to smile. "I saw how well you did last time," he said. "What was that all about, anyway?"

"He saw me with a friend of mine—guy from New York," Steven said. "We—were roommates there."

"Well"—Matthew shrugged, after a moment's thought—"you got over the problem of just being a Carrington. I suppose you'll have to work this one out, too. Big Ed's nothing but trouble. We'd let him go if we weren't so damned shorthanded."

"No," Steven said quickly. "I don't want him—or anybody—fired on my account."

Matthew put his hand on the young man's shoulder. "Good boy," he said quietly. "Say, by the way, you sure impressed my wife the other night. She wants me to invite you home for dinner. Soon as my jaw heals so I can chew a steak. Okay?"

Steven laughed in relief. "Okay," he said. "And— thanks, Matthew."

"I'm driving back to town now," Matthew said. "Want a ride?"

Steven shook his head. "Appreciate it," he said, "but I'm staying in the bunkhouse for a spell."

"Good. See you tomorrow."

It was almost midnight when Blake Carrington came home that night. He greeted his wife first and then strode across the landing to knock on his daughter's door.

"Interruptible?" he asked.

She was reading but looked up with delight. "Seeing how it's you—yes," she said, grinning.

Her father sat down on the chair facing her bed. "Jeff Colby is a hell of a nice boy," he said without preliminaries.

"Is he? He's also a bit of a jerk." She frowned, wondering what this was all about.

"Well, I understand that you kids have strange courting habits these days," her father said cheerily. "But if it works, terrific."

"If what works?" Fallon asked indignantly. "Daddy, what do you mean, courting habits? One courts when one is going to marry."

Blake nodded. "Uh-huh."

Barely keeping rein on her anger, Fallon retorted, "Uh-huh what?" And then she couldn't help but ask, "Did Cecil Colby say something to you?"

"Maybe weddings in this house are becoming a contagious, if benign, disease" was her father's infuriating reply.

"It was Cecil, wasn't it?"

"Well, you could say he kind of—alluded."

"He had no right to say anything to you," Fallon exploded. "It's my life!"

"Whoa," her father cautioned. He stood up and came over to her, to sit down on the edge of her bed and take her hands in his. "Don't be so hard on him," he said. "We were having a few drinks at the club yesterday, and one thing led to another. Look, we won't talk about it if you don't want to. Okay?"

"Let's not," she agreed.

"It's your life," he assured her, "and you go ahead and move at your own pace. But I just want to say that if it does happen, I'll be very pleased. I'll feel very good about it."

Fallon just looked glum, and Blake bent over to kiss her forehead. Then he stood up and said good night and left her to brood and scheme in silence.

The next day, Michael drove her to the Colbyco Building.

"The lady is moping," he observed over his shoulder as he eyed her in the rear-view mirror.

"Mind your damned business and drive," she snapped.

He maneuvered a corner and a stop light. Then he asked, "Am I going to see you tonight?"

"Just drive, please."

He said no more until he got out to hold the door open for her. "Listen," he said, "about tonight. I just remembered—I've got a date."

"Pay her the ten dollars and enjoy," Fallon retorted as she swept past him.

"That'll be the day!" he exclaimed loudly enough for her to hear as she went through the revolving door of the skyscraper.

On the top floor, she demanded to see Mr. Colby at once and was admitted as soon as the secretary gave her name on the intercom.

"Would you like a drink?" he asked her, opening the bar with a remote button from his desk. The low teak cabinet shone with an array of bottles and glasses and several temperature-controlled racks of vintage wines.

Fallon shook her head.

"You're upset," he said. He got up from his desk then and came over to her.

"I had a talk with my father last night. You told him I was going to marry Jeff."

"Why shouldn't I have told him? Isn't it true?"

"Cecil, I've tried to live with this. But I'm not sure I can go through with it. We're so different, Jeff and I—"

"You and I have an agreement," Cecil Colby said softly. He was a man who could quietly assume that people—everyone—would do exactly as he bade them, and he would be right almost every time.

"I know we do," Fallon said, attempting a smile in spite of her misery. "But why can't I marry you?"

It hung in the air.

"Because," the older man said gently, "that wouldn't benefit either of us. And because we made a deal."

"Cecil," she said, her huge blue eyes wide, talking fast to keep away the hopelessness that was creeping up inside her, "I wouldn't be good for Jeff. The two of us together would go very slowly and not so quietly insane. But you and I—we'd be something special. We'd be incredible together."

"Oh, my dear, you tempt me, you really do. But— no. If I put my personal pleasure first, I wouldn't be where I am, would I? No, you and I do what's best in the long run because we're smart. For you, the most important thing was that I bail your father out. And for me, what's best is that you marry my nephew."

"You rejecting me, Cecil?" she asked in a voice so brittle it threatened to break.

"How about that drink now?" he asked smoothly.

"Ram it," she said. She went over to his desk and picked up the phone. Immediately, a secretary answered. "Connect me with Jeff Colby," Fallon said. Her eyes locked with Cecil Colby's, she spoke into the phone. "Take me out to lunch," she ordered. "I'll pick you up in ten seconds." She hung up.

"See you around, Uncle Cecil," she said with the air of Madame Pompadour going to the guillotine. She stopped just short of the door. "Last chance to change your mind?" she offered wryly. When he smiled and shook his head, she went on down the hall to the junior executive suite.

"Hey, you like to gamble?" she asked, poking her head through Jeff's office door.

"Fallon! What a terrific surprise! What are you doing here?"

"Being taken to lunch?"

"Okay, sure. Just let me make a call; have to cancel one of the partners—what do you mean, gamble?"

"Just wondering," she answered vaguely. "This sure is a tiny office compared to your uncle's," she said.

Fourteen hours later, Krystle Carrington heard the sound of loud voices in the hall outside her bedroom door. She shook her husband to wake him. Blake listened, then switched on the bedside lamp.

"Is that Fallon?" he asked, glancing at the clock. Three A.M.

"I think so, but who's she got with her?" Krystle whispered, alarmed.

They crossed the room and opened the door to the vision of a slightly tipsy Fallon half supporting and half being supported by an equally tipsy Jeff Colby. They were laughing.

"Hi, folks!" Jeff said brightly. "We just flew back from Vegas!"

"And we're married." Fallon giggled.

"You're—" A huge smile broke on Blake's face. "Congratulations, baby!" He held out his hand to Jeff. "I'm very glad, Jeff. Very."

"Congratulations," Krystle said warmly to both of them.

"Thanks, Krystle," Jeff answered.

But Fallon only threw herself into her father's arms, clinging tightly. In the shadow of the embrace, Krystle saw Fallon's smile melt into the frightened, defenseless look of a lost little girl.

7

Blake Carrington came out of the shower on Sunday morning feeling better than he had since his honeymoon. All was well with the world, at least for now, and in his bed was the most beautiful—

But the bed was empty. He tied the cord of his terry-cloth robe around himself and called her name. No answer. His eyes fell on a folded sheet of pale-blue stationery on one of the pillows.

"Meet me in the kitchen!"

He laughed and stretched, then checked his image in a mirror and threw open the door to go downstairs.

Krystle, wearing a huge apron over her negligee, was alone in the cavernous room. She was removing a box of eggs from the refrigerator as he came down the steps. He watched her set the box on a butcher-block work table that already held an assortment of ingredients. He recognized green peppers and tomatoes.

"What's going on? Where's the staff?" he asked, amused.

"I sent them packing. Whisk, like that. Gave them the day off." When she saw how he was looking at her, she grinned. "I am, after all, the mistress of the house. At least that's what the man said. Didn't he?"

Blake nodded, thinking to himself how incredibly lucky he was.

"Well, then," Krystle said. "Now, how does the man like his omelette?"

"Very Spanish," Blake answered. He came around behind her and put his arms around her.

"Lots of hot stuff?" she asked, laughing.

"Oh, yes, lots and lots."

He watched her chopping jalapeno peppers. "I love you, Mrs. Carrington," he said.

"And I love you," she told him. "Especially on a day like this, when those lines on your distinguished forehead don't look tight, when you can yell out to the world, "Get lost. I'm taking the day off to be with my wife."

He sat on a stool to watch her. "I feel so relaxed when I'm with you."

"And I'm just happy to see you this way. Now, let me get to work here. I make a pretty mean omelette, or I used to, anyway."

"I'm glad Fallon decided to spend the weekend with her friend Denise. I guess she's lonely with Jeff out of town," Blake said, helping himself to a sliver of tomato.

"Yes. We've got the whole house to ourselves for the whole day," Krystle said happily. She whipped the sauces and seasonings into the eggs. "What would you like to do?"

"Go back to bed," he answered honestly.

Krystle laughed and kissed him and tried to concentrate on cooking.

Sunday dinner at the Blaisdel house was simple and servantless, too. Steven Carrington thought it was the best meat loaf he had ever tasted, and he felt more at home with Matthew and Claudia and their fourteen-year-old daughter than he did in his own home these days.

"Does your wife ever make meat loaf, Steven?" Lindsay Blaisdel asked him.

"I'm not married," he told her.

She was obviously delighted at the news. "Oh, well, I just thought maybe she was out of town or something. . . . you engaged?"

"Lindsay, questions like that aren't very polite," her father said.

"It's okay, Matthew. I'm kind of flattered. No, I'm not engaged, either," Steven told the happy teenager.

"Steven lived in New York for a while," Claudia told her daughter.

Lindsay sighed loudly. "I've always wanted to go to New York," she said. "Tell me about it."

"It's wonderful," he said. "Totally alive, every inch of it, every minute. The best of everything, too—that's where people go to match themselves against the best. Theater and museums and concerts and—oh, bicycling in Central Park and looking at the skyline from the Staten Island Ferry. It's beautiful as well as exciting."

"Why did you come back, then?" the young girl asked.

"Lindsay, really, some things are personal, you know," Matthew said.

"Yes, for personal reasons. To be with my family and because this is where my future is. But I'll go back to New York every chance I get for vacations and to see plays."

"It sounds wonderful." Lindsay sighed.

"But they have a law in New York that says no one admitted who hasn't finished her homework," Claudia said. "Isn't that right, Steven?"

"Oh, Mother!"

"Oh, it's true, Lindsay. Guards at the city limits with laser-ray guns, demanding to see your notebooks before they'll let you pass."

"Okay, okay—may I be excused from the dishes, then?"

"Yes, go ahead."

"I've got some work to do of my own, if you'll excuse me," Matthew said.

Steven helped with the dishes, and while they were getting washed in the machine, he sat in the kitchen laughing and talking with Claudia and eating chocolate chip cookies from a jar.

"Lindsay's got a terrific spirit, and—openness," he said. "I hope she hangs on to that and doesn't get all up-tight like so many people when they grow up."

"It hasn't left you," Claudia said.

"I'm not open," he protested.

"You are," she said quietly. "About important things. Who you are—what you feel. I envy you that."

Steven's smile faded as he realized what she was alluding to. "Matthew told you about me," he said.

"Somebody told me. About you. About the fighting you have to do, the ragging you take. Why don't you leave it, Steven? There are a lot of other things you can do. What are you trying to prove to those men?"

He smiled again. "If I didn't know you as well as I feel I do, I'd think the boss's wife was telling me to pack it in."

"I am. I for one wouldn't think any less of you."

"I'd miss out on another great meat-loaf dinner."

"You'd always be welcome here."

Their eyes locked.

"You'd want me to come?" he asked in a low voice, almost whispering.

"Of course," she whispered back.

His smile widened wistfully. "And—I'd bring flowers next time," he said. "And make thee beds of roses." He cleared his throat. "That's Marlowe, I think. 'A Shepherd To His Love,' I think—or something like that."

Claudia moved her arm in an involuntary spasm behind her. A dish went crashing to the tile floor and broke into fragments.

She bent to pick up the pieces, and he bent to help her, and without a word, on their knees facing each other, they stopped reaching for the bits of broken china and reached for each other.

Their kiss was warm and gentle, not passionate but rising from both their needs. It had a quiet sexuality, a tenderness that spoke for itself.

When they moved apart, they were both embarrassed. Steven rose, saying, "I'd better go." Claudia, still on her knees, her hand bleeding slightly from clutching the broken china shards so tightly, could only nod and let him go.

He went home that night instead of heading back to the rig. Sunday was a day off; no one slept in the bunkhouse on Sunday nights. It would have been an admission that you had no private life or no taste for the wild houses and barrooms. Steven headed for his father's house, thinking that it was time he found an apartment for himself in town, trying not to think about kissing Matthew Blaisdel's wife.

His sister was just pulling into the driveway in Jeff's Mercedes convertible. He followed her lights under the trees and around to the garage. She pulled up, got out, and came over to him. She was wearing a very low cut long gown, diamonds in her ears, and no lipstick.

"Hi," she said, leaning down into his window.

"Hi."

"You going to lecture me?"

"What about?"

"About my husband being out of town and how I should be locked in my room with a Bronte novel?"

Steven grinned at her. "When did I ever tell you how to behave?" he asked. "Move over so I can get out."

She stepped back. The lantern glow from the driveway beacon picked up the glitter of her eyes and earrings and her glossy lips. She had been up to no good, and clearly, she wanted to be challenged. Steven got out of his car and put his arm around her to lead her toward the house.

"Want to play backgammon?" she asked him as they walked.

"No. I'm beat."

"Monopoly? You still owe me a free ride on the railroad of my choosing from the last time we played."

"How about letting a little old tired brother get some sleep?"

"You got a telegram this morning."

Steven opened the door to the solarium and let her through ahead of him. "Where is it?" he asked.

"In your room."

He stopped in mock astonishment. The moonlight came through the glass windows of the solarium, and there was no need to turn on any lights. "You mean you haven't read it yet?"

"Of course not! What do you take me for?"

"Who's it from?"

"Let's go see," she shouted suddenly, slipping out of her high-heeled shoes and leaving them there as she made a dash for the front hall and the staircase. Steven bounded to catch up, and they reached his room in a dead heat, trying not to wake Blake and Krystle with their laughter.

He grabbed the envelope from his desk and slit it open, threatening her with the heavy silver paper knife when she tried to reach for the telegram. He held it at arm's length to read it over Fallon's head. She saw his face fall, the laughter give way to concern.

"What is it? What's the matter, Steven?" Fallon stopped the mock struggle and sank down on a sofa. "Is it from Ted?" she asked.

Steven looked at her and nodded. "Ted. Right," he said.

"And?"

"He wants to come here for a visit. He says he— needs to see me."

"Do you want to see him?" she asked quietly.

Steven sank down onto a wing-back chair that faced the sofa at an angle. "I'm not sure," he replied.

Leaning forward, very serious now, Fallon said, "Steven, do you remember how when you were a boy you had every girl around here doing flip-flops over you?" He shrugged. "What did you feel, as a boy, about those girls?" she pressed him.

He shrugged again, a little impatient. "That they were pretty, some of them."

"Some of them still are," his sister said. "And still doing flip-flops. Have you ever tried with any of them? With any woman?"

Instead of answering, Steven stared at the carpet.

"You haven't, have you? If you don't try it, how can you ever know who you are—or what you are?" she went on, not unkindly.

Now he looked at her. There was pain in his eyes. "Maybe I'll never know, Fallon," he said.

She held out her hand to him, and he took it. "Hey," she said, "I don't know why we're the way we are. We haven't had a mother around for a very long, long time. That could be it. But here I am, the scandal of Colorado. And here you are—"

She stopped.

Steven finished the sentence. "Blake Carrington's mistake," he said, and somehow he found a smile. "We are a pair."

Fallon held on to his hand. "Whatever we are," she said seriously, "I know one thing. You're scared, and I am, too. Lots of stuff still scares me. That I won't amount to anything. That I won't measure up to Blake Carrington. I look at this ring on my finger, and it looks like a noose—hey, Steven, remember how after Mother left, I couldn't fall asleep for six months? How I'd come in here and we'd hold hands in the dark, just like Hansel and Gretel, wondering where she'd gone and why she'd gone and never knowing—and remember how I used to tell you how much I loved you and cared for you? And how we'd always, always be together?"

Steven nodded, too filled with emotion to say anything.

She stood up, leaned over to kiss him tenderly on the

forehead, and whispered, "We will, too. Get some sleep, big brother."

He decided to put off answering Ted for a while. He slept very well—all things considered. His King-sized bed and percale sheets had something over the narrow bunk and mattress ticking for comfort. And the air-conditioned quiet over a bunkhouse full of snoring men—but he was up at four-thirty, refreshed and ready for another hard week.

It was midafternoon when Steven, at the top of the derrick structure, reached out for the bit to brake it with his wrench. He made contact, gave the bit a twist, and felt a sudden lurch and then the sickening sensation of no resistance where there should have been the sturdy kingpin of the rig. Something huge and deadly went flying in one direction, and Steven felt himself plummeting through the air, brought up short by the jolt of his safety belt cutting into his waist and shoulders. He was dangling upside down, his head about six feet from the ground and his feet in the air. Below him, the men were shouting and running away from the debris of iron and tools that were falling from the platform at the top.

"What's going on here?" Matthew Blaisdel ran out of the office shed.

"The bit twisted off!" Steven heard Big Ed shout. "Guess who did it," the rigger went on. From his upside-down vantage point, waiting to be helped down, Steven saw Ed gesture in his direction.

Another rigger, Lenny, chimed in. "Yeah. Big guess. Carrington. It was Carrington."

"Just what we needed, right?" added Buck Wallace. The men had stopped running away and were coming in close now, circling around Matthew and Walter, who had just come up. Steven's head was throbbing. He couldn't believe that they were all just letting him hang there.

"How bad is it?" Walter Lankershim asked.

"We lost the bit," one of the men answered.

"What depth?"

"A good sixty-one hundred. We can try to fish it out, but you know damned well there's no way."

Steven saw Matthew turn toward Big Ed. "Where were you when this happened? You're the driller," Matthew said angrily.

"I was trying to fix the shaker," Ed answered. "I told Carrington to take over the brake. I figured I could trust him for a few minutes."

Matthew turned back to his partner. "How much do you figure it'll cost to fix?"

The older man shook his head. "I'd say thirty thousand, maybe closer to forty these days. Minimum. If everything goes perfect on the first run."

Steven was wishing he could black out, even die. He no longer had any feeling in his arms and legs. Tears were running out of his eyes and falling back onto his forehead and into his thick blond hair.

"We're finished," Walter went on glumly. "We've barely got mud money. Where are we going to get that kind of cash?"

No one answered. No one could. After a long, painful moment, Big Ed and Buck meandered over to the rope that Steven dangled from. They caught hold of it and began to swing it, twirling him around and around. Dizzy, nauseous, guilty, Steven shut his eyes and hoped to die.

"Let him down!" It was Matthew's voice.

"We're gonna leave him there til he admits it—that he done it on purpose," Buck answered back.

"I said cut him down," Matthew repeated. Steven heard him as from a dim and distant place. If he had had the strength, he would have told Matthew not to bother, he wasn't worth saving.

They cranked him slowly to the ground. Steven crumpled helplessly for a moment until the blood came back into his hands and legs and he was able to stand. He hobbled over to Matthew and Walter.

"Got to go to Carrington now or Colby or one of those other hotshots," Walter was saying. "We gotta sell our lease now or close down. No other choices I can see."

"Give us a day, Walter," Matthew answered. "If we've got to go to Carrington or any of the others, at least give us a day to think of another way out."

Walter nodded, and Matthew turned to go down to his Cherokee. He saw Steven standing there and started to brush past him without a word.

"Matthew, honest to God, I didn't do it on purpose," Steven managed to say. His throat was so dry it hurt to talk.

"I think you'd better run along," was all Matthew said.

Steven hesitated, then nodded and limped away.

"And here I was beginning to like the kid," Walter said.

"It could have happened to any of us," Matthew answered.

"Yeah, except he's the guy whose old man's just been waiting to take everything we've been working for."

Steven collected his few things from the bunkhouse and left the rig site. No one spoke to him. He got into his car and drove away. There was no place to go except home.

He showered and cleaned himself up—no visible bruises—and went downstairs to the library where his father and stepmother were having a drink before dinner.

Krystle greeted him with a huge smile. She always seemed genuinely glad to see him. "Steven, how nice! Come have a drink with us."

He shook his head. "Thanks, Krystle. But not just now."

"Thought you were staying out at the rig for a while," Blake said. He was sitting back comfortably on one of the green velvet sofas flanking the fireplace, stretched out and looking satisfied with the whole world.

"We twisted off," Steven said. "We shut down."

"I know," his father said.

Astonished, Steven stared at him. "How do you know?"

"Bad news travels fast," Blake said.

Steven could only stare. His head started to throb again. "Bad news or good news?" he asked coolly.

Blake smiled. "I guess it depends on your point of view."

Steven was aware of Krystle watching him curiously. As if she could see bruises that didn't show on the skin—he shook off the feeling that she was on his side. Why was everybody in this house always having to choose sides?

He looked his father in the eye. "Dad, it was my fault."

Blake set his drink down on the cocktail table. "That

I didn't know," he said calmly. "Well, it could have happened to anyone."

"But it wasn't just anyone," Steven burst out. "It was me. It was my responsibility. They gave me a chance. They trusted me. Matthew was my friend, and now— this was his shot at the big one, his and Walter's, and—" He broke off.

"Breaks of the game," his father said, still calm and unruffled. "Rotten break."

Steve stood there for a moment. His father sipped at his drink. Krystle watched them both, looking with compassion from one to the other, knowing something was between them that she could not reach. After what seemed a very long time, Steven said, "Dad, I want you to give them a chance. I want you to extend their lease time." He stopped himself from saying, "please."

"Why would I do that?" Blake asked with genuine surprise. "You know perfectly well I've been waiting around for those leases. Besides, I've got troubles of my own right now."

"Matthew and Walter didn't cause your trouble. But I did cause theirs." He stopped a minute, took a deep breath, and went on. "If you help them, Dad, I'll do anything you want. I'll come to work for you. I'll try to be—the son you want me to be."

"Oh? Does that mean you'll take a job in my public relations office?"

"Yes, sir."

"Does that mean if I call up Brian Cable and tell him you'd like to date his daughter, you'd go out with her?"

"Yes, sir."

"Does that mean you'll be giving up your—curious New York ways?"

Steven nodded his head. Blake regarded him with narrowed eyes. Then he lashed out angrily. "For Matthew Blaisdel you'd do all that. But not for me."

"Blake—" Krystle broke in, but neither father nor son heard her.

"Dad, I just want you to do what's fair," Steven said.

"Then stop giving me conditions. And be what I want you to be."

Realizing the futility of this argument, Steven turned to leave the room.

"Steven—wait." Blake Carrington was incapable of apologizing, certainly not to his own son. But he came as close now as he could. "I didn't mean to hurt you. And I know you don't mean to hurt me, either. Why do you think I've worked so hard? Who do you think I've built all of this for? I'm not going to be around forever. It's all for you, Steven. I did it all for you and for your sister. For my family."

"I'm sure you thought that's what you were doing, Dad. And I appreciate the thought. I really do. But I'm not the imaginary son you did it for, I guess. And I still need to know—are you going to let Lankershim and Blaisdel go?"

Blake looked old suddenly. Steven felt a chill tremble through his body, still stiff and aching from the morning's ordeal. But he stood his ground and waited for his father's answer.

"No," Blake said finally.

Steven looked at him for one last, frustrated minute and then left the library. Blake got up from the green sofa and went over to his wife, who had moved to the window and stood now, looking out. His hands were cold when he put them on her shoulders.

"You're thinking?" he asked her.

"About how beautiful it is here," she said, staring out at the rolling lawns and the fruit trees, "and how ugly, sometimes."

He kissed her cheek, but she didn't turn to him.

"Blake, he's your son. Your son opened up to you. He threw himself on your mercy. It wasn't easy for him to take the blame for that accident, but he came to you, and you cut him off again. How do you ever expect to be close to him?"

Blake dropped his hands. He stood behind her without touching her. His voice turned distant. "Is it Steven you're concerned about or Matthew Blaisdel?"

She turned and looked at him. "That's a rotten thing to say, Blake."

"Sometimes rotten things have to be said." He turned from her level gaze. He went to the bar and poured himself another vodka on the rocks.

"And rotten things have to be done, too, I suppose," she said, getting angry.

"What does that mean?"

"Matthew was your friend. Up until six weeks ago, he worked his heart out for you, your company—"

Interrupting, Blake said, "And then he quit, walked out on me. End of friendship and loyalty. Period."

"He was trying to make it on his own, finally. The way you did."

"And he's failing."

"And you did everything you could to see that he failed!"

"How the hell did I end up with a family full of bleeding hearts! Can't you at least get it straight that I'm running a practical business and sometimes a dirty one? We can't survive by giving things away. You'd better learn that unless you want Denver-Carrington to be bailed out by Congress—or worse, go under. Survival counts; that's all. Survival. I have to do the dirty stuff so you and Steven can have the luxury of feeling sorry for the ones who aren't so lucky. For Matthew Blaisdel—"

"What do you mean, dirty stuff?"

Blake put his empty glass down. "I've got some telephone calls to make," he said. "I'll see you at dinner. Maybe we'll both be a bit calmer then."

He left the room. Krystle stared after him for a minute. Her anger subsided quickly. She reached for the phone and dialed Joseph.

The major-domo was there in a moment, entering the room after a discreet knock.

"Yes, ma'am?"

"We'll have dinner on the terrace tonight, Joseph. And—some good champagne, and candles in those etched-glass hurricane lamps, please."

"I'm sorry, Mrs. Carrington, but—"

"Joseph. Do you have trouble with your hearing?"

"No, Mrs. Carrington. However—"

"Oh, I'm glad. Then I'm sure we have nothing more to discuss. Thank you, Joseph. That will be all."

"Yes, ma'am."

When he had gone, she looked down at her hands, expecting to find herself shaking, but her fingers were slender, well manicured, and steady. You're learning, she told herself, like it or not.

8

The soft mud came almost to Matthew's knees. His hip boots made a sucking sound with each step he took, cautiously and laboriously, along the collar of the rig, twenty feet below ground level. His flashlight moved slowly along the walls of the rig cellar as he checked every centimeter of the gritty, slimy interior. He had been down there for over an hour when the light caught a reflected gleam of something on one of the flanges of the huge Blow-Out Preventor apparatus. He leaned forward cautiously to take hold of the small object. He put it inside his glove and made his way to the ladder.

Back up on the ground, in the silence of the deserted rig, the cold new moon had slipped out of sight behind the mountains. Matthew pulled off his boots and made his way to the office shed. Inside, under the bare light bulb, he examined his find carefully. It had quite a story to tell.

He headed the Cherokee for the Rigger's Bar, but halfway there Matthew had a better idea of how to find out what he needed to know. He turned off at a boulevard leading to a mobile-home camp. Inquiry at the office sent him past domestic scenes of families finishing their dinners, kids playing ball, and men and women talking pleasantly in the cool evening air. Bobby

Morrow was outside number 164, watering a little patch of grass.

"Hi, Matthew. What're you doin' here? Come on in. You want a beer?"

"No, thanks, Bobby. Maybe we'd better talk out here. I want to show you something."

Lean and muscular, looking out of place in this domestic setting, the young rigger threw down the watering hose and came over to the Cherokee.

"Allen screw, right?" he said, looking at the object in Matthew's hand.

"Right. From the stabilizer, I'd say, wouldn't you?"

Bobby nodded, puzzled. "Yeah, I'd say that's where it came from."

"It's not broken. It was deliberately removed, Bobby. Somebody removed this screw, and the stabilizer pad worked itself loose and fell off. That's what jammed the drill stem," Matthew said. "That bit didn't twist off by accident."

Bobby pursed his lips in a long, low whistle, which stopped short when he realized Matthew was waiting for his reaction. "You're not accusing me, are you?" he asked.

"I'm not accusing anybody yet. But I thought you might happen to know something about it."

Bobby backed off. "I don't," he said.

"You're sure about that? Steven Carrington took the blame for it. You saw what happened this afternoon. I thought maybe you weren't so keen on seeing him take the rap as some of the other guys were."

Bobby shook his head. "If he did it, he did it. Somebody did," he pointed out.

"But I think maybe you know who really did it, am I

right? And you're afraid they'll think you're a fag or something if you come to Steven's defense? Is that it?"

"No, it's not that. I'm not afraid of that—"

"What, then?"

"You know what it's like to rat on someone you have to work with, even if—"

"You do know something. I thought so. You going to be an accessory to the crime, Bobby? Where is your loyalty—to a guy who'd do that?"

Bobby squirmed and sweated and finally looked Matthew in the eye. "Come on inside," he said.

An hour later, Matthew and Big Ed were face to face in the Rigger's Bar. Well, not exactly face to face. Big Ed's face was in a sinkful of dishwater and soaking beer glasses, being held down by Matthew's fist curled around his hair. Every once in a while, Big Ed was let up for a gulp of air and a question.

"Who paid you to twist us off?"

"You're crazy, man! Let go of me!"

Dunk.

"Who?"

"Nobody! It was—it was my own idea, okay?"

Dunk.

"Who, damn it? Who?"

Sputter and gasp. "Ugh—Carrington! Carrington's people."

He was pulled from the sink and allowed to go sprawling on the floor. "I don't ever want to see that miserable mug of yours again. You hear?" Matthew turned to the other men at the bar. "One way or another, we're going to get up and running again. The rest of you are welcome back to work when we do."

He left the bar and drove straight to Blake Carrington's

mansion up on the mountain side. It was late now, nearly midnight, but he announced himself at the gate and was admitted. Driving the curved road up toward the house, he had only a moment to hope fervently that Krystle would be out or asleep when he had his confrontation with her husband.

Joseph opened the door to him, wordlessly but eloquently appraised Matthew's work clothes, and led him into the library. Krystle was halfway up the stairs, on her way to bed, when he came in. She stopped, but he did not look up to see her.

But she heard his first words to Blake before the library door closed behind him.

"I want to know what kind of man would let his son take the rap for something his father set up—"

Suddenly out of wind, she sat down on the carpeted step and clutched the polished banister for support. She couldn't believe it; she couldn't. It would be the lowest form of disloyalty to believe Matthew Blaisdel's angry words against her husband's integrity, but in her sinking heart, something told her it was true.

Krystle pulled herself up and wearily climbed the rest of the steps to her room. She had a long hot bath, soaking in the aromatic bubbles and trying not to think about what she' had overheard.

When Blake came upstairs, he seemed nervous and preoccupied. She lay quietly on her side of the bed and watched him pacing, sitting down to untie a shoe, then getting up and walking again, to his bureau, to the dressing room, to the closet, and back to the chair to unlace the other shoe. Suddenly, he sat down at the little round table and picked up the telephone. He punched in a number and waited, drumming his fingers.

Krystle found herself closing her eyes, pretending to be asleep.

"Andrew? Oh, I see—well, please wake him. This is Blake Carrington calling—sorry to disturb you, Andrew, but I need my lawyer's help. Matthew Blaisdel and Walter Lankershim are threatening to bring suit for an accident that happened out at their rig. There's a guy who might say I had something to do with it—just a sourdough, a rigger—they call him Big Ed. He's got a grudge and might say I paid him to—that's right. I want him out of town and out of the state, and permanently. Take care of it, Andy—you know what to do—right—good night."

He hung up the telephone and threw off his other shoe. When he climbed into bed, Krystle huddled on her own side and hoped he wouldn't touch her.

The next morning, after he had gone, she called her friend Doris and arranged to meet for lunch at the salad bar where they used to go regularly.

"You've worked for all the department heads in the company. I know you've handled a lot of private things for them, Doris."

"Oh, yeah, well, sure. Why are you asking—not going to try to get me to tell anything I shouldn't, I know that. What's up, Krys?"

"Well, I know you know about the companies where you can have jewelry copied so well that even the owner can't tell the difference between the original and the copy."

"The fake, you mean. Yeah, I know about stuff like that." Doris was looking at Krystle with undisguised curiosity now, even forgetting to eat as she tried to fathom what could be behind her friend's questions.

The thought of those baseball-sized earrings that had made their appearance at the bridal shower crossed Doris's mind, but that was crazy.

"And I know you know places where a person can get cash discreetly by putting up certain items of value," Krystle went on nervously.

"Krystle, what's this about?"

"I—have something I want to—uh, exchange. To sell, I mean. Doris, you'll help me, won't you? Without ever breathing a word?"

"Well—sure, Krys, but—how come? I mean—I thought you had everything."

"Will you help me?"

"Oh, Jeezus—I think I just figured out what it's about. It's Matthew Blaisdel and his trouble with that rig, isn't it? You're gonna raise cash for him, bail him out?"

Krystle just nodded, biting her lower lip and pleading with her eyes. She had made no pretense of eating the huge leafy green salad in front of her. All around them, workers on their lunch breaks laughed and talked in their own little worlds, while heavy silence fell between Krystle and Doris.

Doris took a bite of raw spinach sprinkled with bacon bits and thought hard as she chewed. Finally, she asked her friend quietly, "Which one of them are you in love with?"

"What do you mean?" Krystle asked, taken by surprise.

"You're doing this for Matthew, right?" Krystle didn't answer. "And Blake knows nothing about it; otherwise you wouldn't be hocking your jewels." Still no reaction from Krystle. "So which of them are you in love with?" Doris repeated.

"I love my husband."

Doris said nothing. She just put down her fork and waited. Finally, Krystle went on. "I find that—I just can't wipe out the fact that there was a Matthew in my life. I thought it was all over between us, or I never would have married Blake, believe me—it is all over between us, of course. But—well—he needs help, and I feel an obligation, that's all."

"I'll bet Blake did something rotten and you're trying to make up for it."

"You're talking about my husband."

"Sorry."

"Will you help me, Doris?"

The waitress put the check down between them. Krystle reached for it, but Doris's hand was quicker. She turned it over to look at the face of it. Then she said, "You know, I've been kind of envious of you. And a little sorry for myself, living in a studio apartment, eating TV dinners, driving around in that old Chevy. But right now I wouldn't change places with you for all of the big houses, the limousines, the caviar in the world."

"Give me the check," Krystle said quietly.

"Okay." Doris let her take it. "The man who buys jewels is a Mr. Volkert, on Bluff Street. He'll make the fake copy for you, too. I'll go with you, I still got time on my lunch hour. Come on."

Mr. Volkert's shop was on the other side of town from the Denver-Carrington Building. Determined, but scared, feeling like a character in a spy movie, Krystle parked down the street about a block away from the discreet sign that proclaimed: "Volker's Antiques, estates bought and sold, appraisals, fine jewelry our specialty."

When Krystle took the enormous egg-shaped emerald from her purse, Mr. Volker started to gulp, turned it into a polite cough, and remarked on the perfection of the clear green stone.

"Now, before we discuss money," he said, stroking his short white beard, "there is only one rule here. If at the end of six months' time you don't return the money, plus of course the interest, the necklace is no longer yours. This is understood?"

Krystle nodded. "I understand," she said quietly.

Mr. Volkert smiled kindly. "You don't look entirely convinced," he said.

"It just seems so—easy, somehow. I mean—" Krystle was not sure what she meant herself. She tried to return his smile, without much success.

"But why not easy?" the pawnbroker said. "People need money for different reasons. Some have habits—that take them to Las Vegas, shall we say? Some have other kinds of habits, even more expensive—none of which is any of my business, you see. None at all."

"How much do I get for it?" she asked nervously.

Mr. Volkert examined the emerald again, caressing it in his hand as he turned it under the light. "I can give you forty thousand dollars," he said finally.

Krystle gasped at the thought of such an expensive object in her possession. She had no idea, but before she could say anything, Mr. Volker spoke again.

"I know, I know," he said, shaking his head. "That's only approximately two-thirds of its market value. However, if you could take it someplace else, you would already have done so."

He started to hand back the emerald on its golden chain, but Krystle did not reach for it.

"Get the money," she said quietly.

Krystle dropped Doris back at the office and drove directly to Matthew Blaisdel's drill site. The rig was silent and still, and no one seemed to be there. She parked and made her way to the office shed. When she knocked on the door, Matthew's voice called out a curt "Come in!"

"Hello, Matthew."

"Krystle—" He looked tired. There was a stack of papers in front of him. He just looked at her and kept on looking.

"May I come in?" she asked, suddenly self-conscious.

He nodded.

Closing the door behind her, Krystle came in and stood alongside his desk. The air was cold out here, and she shivered, unconsciously huddling deeper inside her lynx jacket.

"I hear you've had some trouble," she said.

He gestured widely toward the closed-down, empty rig outside. "See for yourself," he said with a wry grin.

Krystle reached inside her purse and brought out a large envelope, which she handed to him. Matthew took it with a puzzled expression and looked inside. His hand came out with a fat stack of crisp hundred-dollar bills.

"What's this all about?" he asked suspiciously.

"Nothing to do with Blake, believe me," she said quickly. "I know you need it, and I can afford it. So take it. And before you say no, remember—you have a wife and a daughter and a partner and a bunch of men who are all depending on you to bring this well in. So you just take it, and you fish out that drill bit, and you pay me back when you can!"

Matthew stared at her. His hand held the money loosely; his eyes searched hers in a tumult of emotions that all had to be denied. Finally, he nodded slowly. "I'll get it back to you as soon as I can," he said.

"I'm all right for six months," she told him.

"I know Blake wants me out of here. We both know it. Why are you doing this?" he asked her.

"Don't ask me that, Matthew, please. I have my reasons."

"Yes, of course you do. I'm sorry. No questions," he said. He got up from the desk and came around to stand inches from her. The words he said then came involuntarily from his lips. "I love you. Oh, God, how I love you."

"I love you," she answered simply.

They kissed, urgently. He moved with her toward the cot against the wall. They kissed again, and she felt herself melting. With a strength she didn't know she had, she pulled herself out of his embrace.

"I can't, Matthew—I can't give you anything else that's his." She looked longingly at Matthew, who nodded painfully, and then she left, almost running in her haste to save herself.

Matthew stood paralyzed for a long, long moment, not wanting to disturb the sense of her being there, the aura of her presence still hovering in that bare little office and in his aching, empty arms. He heard her Mercedes drive off until there was no more sound. Finally, he stepped back to his desk and sat down. He couldn't go home to Claudia just yet, not with the imprint of Krystle in his brain. He dialed his home number.

"Claudia, I'm going to be late. I'm sorry."

"Oh, well, I'm sorry, too. Matthew?"

"What?"

"Please forgive me, but—well, I just don't understand why you're so busy now, with the rig closed
down. Seems to me there wouldn't be very much to do
at all."

"Damn it, Claudia. I've got to try to save this whole
thing, all on my own. Walter's given up and ready to
sell the lease—oh, never mind!"

"I'm sorry, Matthew. It's all right. Oh, Lindsay had
something she wanted to ask you, but she's gone to an
overnight party at Janey's house. I guess it'll keep. I
guess we both will."

He hung up feeling lousy. Why couldn't he tell his
wife that everything was going to be okay now, that
they'd found a source for a loan? He wouldn't have had
to say who the source was. He could have told her the
truth—that he was going to West Junction to the bank,
then to find Walter and tell him the good news, and
then round up the men and maybe celebrate, but
somehow he had not. He stared at the telephone
ruefully, then grabbed the envelope and his hat and got
out of there.

Claudia hated herself for crying. It was just that she
was so damned lonely. Echoes of her psychiatrist's
advice came back to her. *All right,* she said to herself, *I
won't sit here feeling sorry for myself, and I won't be
alone, either. I'll get as pretty as I can and go out and
see people; that's all I need.*

But where does one go? She had heard about singles
bars, and though she wasn't single, she was alone, and
it was supposed to be perfectly proper to go to those
places. The one she picked had a bright, cheerful sign

out in front and sounds of loud rock music coming out. She sat at the bar and ordered a martini.

Immediately, she was aware of the eyes of several men turned in her direction, assessing her and judging. She wanted to disappear, to crawl out of there. What a mistake; better to be home crying.

"Hi," someone said at her elbow.

She turned to look at him. A pleasant face, in his midthirties, heavy-set but not unattractive. There didn't seem to be anything threatening about him at all.

"Hello," she answered shyly.

"First time here?" he asked, smiling.

Claudia nodded.

"Hey, haven't we met somewhere before?" he asked, as if he had no idea what a dumb thing that was to say.

"No," she answered shortly. She wished he would leave her alone, that they would all leave her alone. She would be contented enough to sit there and sip her drink and just listen to the music and watch all the people without having to talk to any of them.

"Guess you've never been to Detroit," the man was going on and on. "Great city." He moved in closer to her and lowered his voice so that only she could hear it under the blasting, pounding roar of the music. "Wanna hear more about it?" he asked conspiratorially. "I mean about what really goes on in Grosse Point?"

"Not particularly," she said.

He paused for a moment and then nodded and moved off.

She lifted the martini to her lips and discovered that her hand was shaking. A few drops spilled on their way to her mouth. She took a deep swallow.

"You have good taste." A handsome young man with a

friendly voice and frank blue eyes had taken the place of the other fellow. He was grinning as he gestured over his shoulder. "That guy's a creep," he said. "A bona-fide, certified, double-digit-IQ creep. The sovereign state of Michigan's gift to creepdom. Now, on the other hand, I am known as generally likeable, not too bad looking, a whiz at my job, which happens to be a junior executive with Marlin Cosmetics, and whose name happens to be Lawrence Armstrong. Larry to my friends, old and new. And your name is?"

"Claudia."

At which Larry turned to the bartender and called out, "Paul. You'll be so kind as to put Claudia's drinks on my bill."

"Will do," the bartender sang out.

Larry took his glass and clinked it against Claudia's. He smiled, and she found herself smiling back. They drank. Then they danced and laughed a lot and drank some more.

She had no idea how many minutes or hours later it was when she found herself in Larry's Corvette, pulling into the garage of an apartment building in a part of the city she didn't know. He turned off the key and got out, then came over to open the passenger door for her. As she stepped out, he took her into his arms and kissed her.

Everything went around in dizzying circles, and she pushed herself away from him. "Don't! Please!"

"Hey, come on," Larry said, with his best smile. "Ease up. I'm sorry if I came on too fast. Let's go upstairs and have a drink, okay?"

"No," she said. She was terrified.

"I don't get it? We spent the whole evening together.

We danced, and—what was the point? I thought we were having a good time—kind of felt something for each other." He was wheedling, almost whining.

Claudia shook her head. "It was a mistake," she said. "I'm sorry."

"Oh, shit," Larry said, dropping the smile. He was a spoiled kid who couldn't have a toy he wanted to play with.

"I'm married," Claudia explained.

"So am I," he answered. "What difference does that make?"

She just trembled and stood there in the semidarkness of an alien street light.

"What the hell are you? Some kind of tease?" Larry burst out angrily. Claudia turned from him and ran, not knowing where she was going, just away from him. He didn't try to follow. She heard him slam the car door and swear. She kept running.

Unfamiliar houses, apartment buildings, and garages lined both sides of the street. She had no idea how to get home from here, how to get anywhere. She looked around for a bus stop. There was a telephone booth at the corner. Claudia ran into it and slammed the door shut as if someone were after her, as if that accordion door would keep anyone out. The phone worked when she picked up the receiver and put it to her ear; it was a relief just to hear the dial tone. But—who to call?

A number came into her head, unlisted in the Denver phone book but locked into her memory. In the days when her husband had worked for Blake Carrington, the number had been posted on the wall over his desk. Claudia dialed and asked, in a scared and breathless voice, to speak to Steven.

"It's Claudia—Claudia Blaisdel. I'm—I'm in trouble, Steven. And I didn't know who else to call."

He was there in ten minutes. Gratefully, she stepped out of the phone booth and slid into the seat beside him. As he drove, she told him, hesitatingly, what had happened. Steven said nothing, but patted her hand and nodded understandingly as she talked. He drove to the lake, where they got out of the car and walked. The night was cool and clear, and the air blowing off the lake was invigorating and clean. They walked without talking, hand in hand.

"I don't know what came over me—that bar—that man. I've never done anything like that," she said after a while. She was calm now and sober.

"But you didn't do anything," Steven reassured her.

"I almost did," she said, shivering. He put his arm around her. "Feeling better?" he asked.

"I feel safe with you," she said. Then she realized how that sounded and looked sideways up at his face to make sure she hadn't hurt his feelings. She tried to amend her words. "I don't mean safe. I feel, well—safe."

They both laughed. "Even after I tried to hit on you?" he asked, not altogether jokingly.

"Oh, Steven," Claudia said, suddenly feeling old and wise, "a stolen kiss in a messy kitchen following a dinner of meat loaf, mashed potatoes, and chocolate chip cookies is hardly an affair, and besides—"

"What?" he asked.

"I took it as—well, as a strictly brotherly kiss."

"Did you?"

She stopped walking and looked at him. The moonlight reflected like a promise on the calm, clear surface of the lake. It cast a soft aura around Steven's face and his earnest eyes, searching hers. "Yes, I did, Steven. It was sweet, and it was—I don't know—sensitive, like you. You're very sensitive to other people, their feelings. You mustn't ever lose that."

Steven nodded slowly. Their heads were very close together. He wasn't smiling. He looked so vulnerable, so handsome and loving. She thought it was a trick of the moonlight. "It's very late," she said softly. "I'd better get home. You should, too."

"No, I'm heading on up to Manchester Lake tonight. We have a cabin there. I like to be there sometimes, just by myself."

"It sounds lovely." She sighed. "I wish I could go up there with you. Come on, we'd better—"

She tried to turn back to the car, but he stopped her. And then his arms were around her, and she was holding on to him tightly, and this time the kiss was not so gentle, sweet, or innocent.

"Come with me, right now," he whispered in her ear. "I don't want to be alone any more than you do. Come with me, Claudia."

She looked at him, trying to know how to say no. But she took his face in her hands, kissed him again, and whispered yes instead.

9

Edward the butler and several maids scurried down the main staircase carrying suitcases and books tied with cord, stereo equipment, and records.

"You can leave that all here," Steven said from the open doorway. He had just driven his truck around to the front of the house and bounded inside with all the energy of his young years and the early hour of the morning. "I'll load it into the truck myself," he went on cheerfully. "Thank you."

It was almost done. He hoisted the last carton to his shoulder, picked up a large suitcase, and turned back to the door. His father and stepmother, dressed in riding clothes, stood framed in the open doorway, staring at him.

"Good morning, Steven," Krystle said. Her smile was sunny and warm for him.

"Morning, Krystle." He looked at his father.

"Just what are you up to?" was Blake's greeting.

"I left you a note, Dad. About a few personal things I want to fill you in on. For one, I'm moving out of the house." He stood there, still holding the carton high on his shoulder and still gripping the heavy suitcase.

"I can see that," Blake answered icily, not moving

from the doorway. Krystle had stepped inside, but Blake still blocked Steven's way.

"Moving where, Steven?" she asked gently.

He turned to her and let his cheerfulness bubble up again. "A three-room apartment on Kensington. It's over some stores. But it's nice, roomy. You know, high ceilings, tall windows."

"Not like your cramped quarters here," his father put in sarcastically.

Steven sighed. He put down the suitcase and shifted the weight of the carton from one shoulder to the other. "I chose Kensington because it's close to the university," he said.

"Ah. You going to tell me that you've decided you need more schooling? Exactly how much Shelley and Keats does a twenty-four-year-old man need?"

"I want to take an extension course in business administration," Steven answered evenly. "The petroleum end in particular. Work toward a master's."

Blake eased up visibly. "Is that true?" he asked, peering at his son.

A strand of butter-colored hair fell across Steven's face as he leaned down to set the carton on the carpet. He brushed it back and straightened up. "Yes," he said. "And I got a job yesterday. I start tomorrow."

"Oh, really? Did Matthew Blaisdel take you back, after all?"

"He asked me to come back, yes. But I said no. This job is with an outfit called Denver-Carrington."

His father took a minute to digest that. "Public relations?" he asked.

Steven shook his head. "No. At the refinery. I had a

talk with the manager. He asked about my qualifications.
I told him about my experience at the Blaisdel-Lankershim
rig, and he seemed to think I'd do as an apprentice. I
guess it was a combination of my knowledge of Shelley
and Keats, my hard-earned calluses, and the fact that
my old man owns the company that convinced him I
should have the job."

"Good—good," Blake said reluctantly. He had been
standing with the sun at his back, so that his son had to
squint to see him. Consciously or unconsciously, and
Blake Carrington seldom did anything without premed-
itation, he now gave up this psychological advantage
and stepped inside. The two faced each other on a more
equal footing.

"I'm very glad to hear it," Blake went on. "But I
don't know why you have to drive out there every day.
There's plenty of room—"

"At the office," Steven finished for him, smiling.
"Dad, I want to do it the way you did it. I want to get
my hands real dirty, my muscles really aching—sweat
and get dog-tired and fall into bed nights knowing that
I'm learning, really learning this business. The way you
did."

Blake looked at him with something between astonishment, doubt, and pride. He held out his hand.
Steven responded with his own, and they touched for
the first time in months, or years. It was a gentleman's
handshake, not exactly warm but a beginning.

"I'm pleased, really pleased," Blake said. His voice
was a pitch lower than usual due to an unaccustomed
feeling of lumpishness in his throat.

Steve was grinning. He turned to Krystle. She leaned
up to kiss him, and then he quickly shouldered his box

and grabbed his suitcase and went out the open door to his truck.

"He's very happy," Krystle said, turning to go upstairs. "And so are you. You know what I think? I think something's happening in Steven's life. I'd bet he's got himself a girl."

Blake put his arm around her, and they started up the steps together. "That would be too much for one day," he said wryly. "I'll settle for the job. And I'm glad he's moving out, too. A man should be on his own—get something for him, will you? A housewarming gift— something terrific, something romantic. For when he's entertaining his girl, if your intuition is to be believed."

"All right," Krystle agreed.

"Now if I can just get the other one sorted out," Blake mused, half to himself, as they entered their bedroom. He threw off his riding jacket and sat down to tug at his boots.

"I wish I could get close to Fallon," Krystle said sadly. "What's wrong with her, Blake?"

"Nothing," he answered shortly. "Nothing I can't handle."

Privately, Krystle thought that Fallon's husband, not her father, should be 'handling' her, but she said nothing.

Fallon was upset about her brother's leaving. The night after Steven moved out, she and Jeff had one of their awful arguments. They never seemed to have conversations; talk turned to argument, and arguments usually became fights. Too often Jeff ended up spending the night on the sofa in the sitting room off their bedroom, which had once been Fallon's nursery. He would wake up with only the button eyes and outstretched arms of his wife's old Pooh Bear for company. Some mornings Jeff caught himself wondering whose side Bear was on.

He never knew what would set Fallon off. This time it was because he had suggested that they, too, should move out of this house.

"Why?" she asked immediately. "Can you give me one good reason why?"

"I can give you plenty," he said. He started to hope that the discussion would stay rational, but he should have known better.

"We have everything we want here, right here in this house," she said. The danger signals were rising. Her alabaster skin was tinged with pale pink, and her eyes raged like wintry green seas. She tossed her hair, and her lips formed a pout when they had done with their cold words.

"Steven got out," Jeff reminded her. He was determined to stay calm.

"Steven had his reasons."

"So do I, Fallon. Can't you understand that?"

"No, I can't," she snapped. She turned from him, went over to her dressing table and switched on the rows of makeup lights. She leaned into the glass, and he saw the angry glint of her eyes reflected back at him over and over in the myriad mirrors.

"Look, I love you," he persisted, "but I don't feel comfortable living here, living under your father's roof. I did it as—well, as a favor to you at first—a sort of wedding present, because I knew you weren't ready to leave. Because I knew it was what you wanted. But now it's time for us to start our own lives. We could have a wonderful life in New Orleans—"

"New Orleans!"

"Yes, there's a chance for me to take over one of the offices, be my own boss. That's where I want to be, with you. We could find a house on the lake—or wherever you want. Just the two of us—"

Fallon took off her earrings and dropped them on the marble top of her dressing table. Then she removed her rings one by one and dropped them with a series of clatters. Then she said, "I hate those swamps."

Jeff's voice rose. "What do you like, Fallon? What? Look, I'm not stupid. I'm not as stupid as you think I am. I mean, I knew you weren't madly in love with me, but I think I had a right to expect—"

"Jeff, will you please keep your voice down." It was not a question but an order. It was always this way. She was the calm one, not he, because she felt nothing, and he was desperately, overwhelmingly, insanely, in love.

In a softer voice, he tried to explain. "I didn't come into this with my eyes closed. And I know there were other people in your life before me. There were other people in mine. And I convinced myself that was not important. I just felt that, for now, I loved you enough for both of us. And that somehow I could make you care for me the way I cared for you—" He stopped, waiting for her reaction, but there was none. She sat impassively and listened, watching him in her mirror.

"Are you even listening to me?" he asked finally, filled with hopelessness and futile rage.

"Do we have to talk about this now?" she answered. She sounded bored.

"That's just the point!" Jeff said. He stood up and began pacing the pale Aubusson carpet between the fireplace and the little breakfast table in the window alcove. "How can we go on living here, in a place where you want me to whisper about things inside me, things I'm feeling, so that they won't hear, so that he won't hear!"

"What are you talking about?"

"You know what I'm talking about! Anybody who knows you knows what I'm talking about! You don't want to upset your father; you want only to please your father. Because more than anything else on this planet, you love your father! And I'm the unlucky substitute, that's all. Too bad you had to marry me; you should have married him!"

Fallon stood up. She turned to stare at him, and he stopped pacing, pinned by her green eyes. She broke off the furious stare to walk across the room and out onto the landing. He ran after her but didn't call out for fear of waking Blake and Krystle. Fallon ran down the stairs and out the front door. Jeff listened for the sound of her car, but it never came. Lying wide awake in her pink and ivory bed, Jeff tried to convince himself that his wife had re-entered the house through another door and was sleeping in one of the guest rooms in the opposite wing.

"I know something you'd like to know," Michael said indolently, drawing his index finger slowly up and down Fallon's bare back.

"You been eavesdropping again? What a sneak," she answered, her voice muffled from the depths of his pillow.

"Takes one to know one," he murmured, nuzzling the words into the back of her neck, the soft, damp, private spot underneath her hair.

Fallon raised herself up on an elbow and looked at him quizzically. "What I do is my business and what you do is my father's business. I hope you don't think you're smart enough to put anything over on him."

"Don't know what you mean," he said. Pleased with himself, Michael rolled over on his back and stretched his bare arms over his head. He yawned. "You think your father knows everything—about his wife, for instance? Believe me, he doesn't. I might have a thing or two to tell him one of these days that could come as big news."

Fallon sat up. She stared down at his mocking blue eyes and the rising bruise on his upper lip where she had bitten him in passion a few moments before. "Are you blackmailing my father?" she asked suddenly.

Michael grinned and shrugged. "A boy's got to get ahead any way he can," he said. He reached out his lazy fingers to tickle her flesh just at the side where her breast began to swell.

Fallon pulled away from him. She reached for her dress and slipped it over her head. Standing barefoot beside the bed, loathing him for his damned self-satisfied grin, she tossed her black curls and said impatiently, "Okay, what do you know that I don't, smartass?"

Michael laughed. "Where are you going this time of night? Back to your husband? Come on over here. You don't want to go anywhere. Not yet."

Fallon hesitated. "Do I have to buy the information from you?" she asked angrily. "How much?"

The chauffeur was very pleased with himself. "I might whisper it in your ear if your ear was close enough," he teased.

"Why would you tell me for nothing when you think you could sell the information to my father for cash?" she asked coldly.

"You really want to know? Because I tried that once. Your father doesn't buy. No, I could go to my grave with this hot information just my secret and Krystle's."

"Mrs. Carrington to you," Fallon said automatically. Her mind was racing—did he really know something? Would it be something useful for her to know, a trump card she could produce if Krystle got too big for her britches. Fallon was not above a little blackmail herself, she realized with an involuntary little smile.

Michael assumed the smile was for him. He moved over to make room for her on the bed. Fallon stared down at him.

"Tell me first," she said.

"Will you spend the night with me if I do—the whole night?"

"Deal."

"What about Jeff?"

"Mr. Colby to you," she answered, and this time her smile really was for Michael. "And the hell with him," she said.

"And your father?"

"I'll make sure he doesn't see me coming back to the house. Now either tell me what you know or I'm splitting, right now."

Michael sat up and reached for a cigarette. Fallon waited impatiently while he lit it, dragged on it, and finally began to tell her how he had been waiting idly outside the Denver-Carrington Building one noon time. It was at least a couple of months ago now, but he hadn't had a chance to see Fallon alone, had he, to tell

her—anyway, he had had a couple of hours to kill
before Blake would need him. He had seen Krystle and
her friend Doris come out of the salad bar next door,
and impulsively he had decided to follow them, just for
the hell of it, a game, a way to kill time. When he told
Fallon where they had gone and the transaction he had
seen through the plate-glass window of the pawnbroker's
shop, she didn't believe him at first. But as she slipped
back into his bed, thinking about what he had described,
Fallon realized that she just might have the dynamite
that was needed to blow Krystle Jennings Carrington
right out of the water.

She threw herself onto Michael's hard, muscular
body with such passion that he soon felt more than
amply rewarded for his cleverness. The two young
animals pounded and drove each other with their own
needs deep into the night.

And out at the Blaisdel-Lankershim rig, even at three
A.M., everything was going full blast, at a tense pitch of
excitement. Every light that could be rigged was blasting
around the rig, focused on the rim and the sludge as it
pumped over the sides, slick black ooze mixing in
slowly and then more regularly with the sand and dirt.
The tank and drill and pumps were the only sounds,
the steady, regular pulsing beat of the machinery as it
pounded and probed and came nearer every second to
the payload.

The men spoke in hushed voices, as pilgrims might
while waiting for a miracle.

"You know what I'm gonna do if it really happens?"

"Yeah, what?"

"Get me a new sports car or a stereo, one of the best.
The very best."

"Your kids would love that. Nice and loud, fill up the house with punk rock!"

"Yeah, you're so right. Make it the sports car, then."

"Me, I'm gonna take a real vacation. Someplace with an ocean."

"God, I'm nervous. Nervous as hell. It's the same every job, if they come this close at all."

"Right, you said it." Murmurs of hushed agreement sat edgily on top of the tension.

Suddenly, a louder noise, different—a sound of gurgling. All eyes went to the shaker tank. In the glare of the concentrated lights, the bubbling fluid began to show unmistakable veins of thick, rich, shiny, black oil.

Walter Lankershim put his finger tips into the sticky ooze and held them to his nose. "Yep," he said, grinning. The shout began to go up, cut off in midair by an accident—the happiest accident in the business. Bits of rotary machinery flew upward, broken, and pushed hundreds of feet into the night air by the pressure of thousands of gallons of oil rushing for the surface in a powerful geyser. Oil splattered down on all the crew, who were momentarily stunned and then ecstatic.

"We hit it! We hit it! Hooray! We did it!"

Black-stained faces and sticky hands gestured and danced around the rig for a moment; then all hands pitched in to cap the well.

Fallon waited in Michael's room over the garage until he had put on his uniform and gone to drive her father to work. She had already watched her husband come from the house, enter the garage, and drive away in his own car. She came down the outside staircase to the circular driveway and crossed the lawn. Slipping past the entry that opened into the kitchen, she took the back stairs two at a time, barefoot, carrying her shoes. It wasn't that Fallon gave a damn for anyone's opinion of her behavior, but this was no time to offer her enemy a choice of weapons.

Half an hour later, freshly showered and changed, a cheerful Fallon joined her stepmother at breakfast in the family dining room.

"Good morning!" She bent close to Krystle as she passed, but only to pick up the delicate little glass bell and give it a quick shake. Krystle looked up and smiled. She immediately folded her newspaper away.

"Good morning, Fallon," she answered warmly.

The maid appeared and took Fallon's order for a very hearty breakfast—"sausages and waffles with whipped cream and a fresh, gigantic pot of coffee, please, Isabel!" —and then Fallon turned her smile and her innocent eyes to Krystle again.

"Daddy gone yet?" she asked.

"Yes. He and Jeff left about a half hour ago."

"Just us girls left behind, huh?"

"Looks that way." Krystle smiled.

"So what are you wearing tonight, Krystle? I mean, so that we don't clash, heaven forbid."

Krystle had to stop and think—what night was this? "Oh, you mean the Randolph party? Your father and I decided not to go," she said. "There are just too many invitations and—"

"I know," Fallon chimed in sympathetically. "I don't blame you. They're really boring people. But I promised Lenore we'd show up."

The maid brought Fallon's freshly squeezed orange juice and set it down before her. Fallon sipped at it.

"Can I ask a favor of you?" she said, wiping her mouth delicately with her napkin.

"Of course," Krystle said, wary but pleased. At least they were talking, and it could signal the beginning of an easier relationship. Since Fallon's marriage, she had been hoping that things would calm down and even grow friendly between the two of them.

"Can I borrow your necklace to wear? The emerald job? Just for tonight?"

She turned her huge, green, innocent eyes on Krystle and waited for her answer.

Krystle felt the blood in her veins freeze for an instant and then begin to flow again. She hoped she hadn't shown anything on her face. Her smile seemed intact. "Of course," she said as smoothly as she could.

"Oh, good. Thanks," Fallon said. Her waffles were set before her, and she began to spoon daubs of thick whipped cream from the silver bowl onto them.

"If you'll excuse me," Krystle said, and Fallon nodded absently, reaching for the folded newspaper.

Upstairs in her dressing room, Krystle opened the wall safe with shaky hands. She reached inside to take out the wrapped, taped package that hadn't been opened since she had placed it there. She clutched at it for a minute, then resolutely tore the paper off the package and opened the black velvet box. Inside, on a bed of white silk, the false emerald lay with its gold chain surrounding it. She held it in her hand. It looked exactly like the original to her eye. She could only hope that it would fool other eyes more accustomed to seeing the real thing.

Fallon knocked on the door before she had disposed of the paper or replaced the emerald in its box. "Just a minute," she called out. Going to the door, she shoved the incriminating paper under her bed, kicking it as far as it would go. She had the box in her hand as she opened the door to her stepdaughter.

"Oh, you got it out for me. How sweet."

Krystle handed Fallon the box wordlessly.

"You're sure you don't mind?" Fallon asked sweetly. She opened the box and took out the necklace.

"No, of course not," Krystle said.

Fallon went to her father's bureau and stood before his mirror. She held the huge green pendant against her bosom. Then she put the chain around her neck and fastened the clasp. Pretending to look at herself in the mirror this way and that way, she was really watching Krystle's reaction.

"What do you think?" she asked. Without waiting for an answer, she went on with girlish enthusiasm. "Wait 'til Lenore comes down the stairs wearing those river pebbles she calls emeralds. She'll make Fitzie sell the Corniche and fly to South America for replacements."

No answer came from Krystle, who had sat down on the edge of the chaise longue and was watching her. "You know," Fallon went on, still chatty, "I can remember the very first time I saw this, Krystle. When I went shopping with Daddy before the wedding. He said he wanted to get something special for you that you'd never want to part with, and he asked me to come help him decide. I saw this, and I said 'right.' That little number could turn any woman into a princess."

"Fallon," Krystle said, and she sounded weary and almost resigned, "you were in Europe when Blake bought me that necklace."

Fallon laughed briefly and tapped herself on the head

to indicate forgetfulness, but not apology or regret. "Was I?" she said, "Of course I was. I must be confusing it with something else. Getting old."

With that, she unclasped the necklace and dropped it into its box. She snapped it shut and handed it back to Krystle. "Here," she said, "I really can't borrow it. I mean, it's yours—just sparkling with sentiment and love and God knows what."

With the kind of calm that comes when emotions hit rock bottom, Krystle asked, "Fallon, is there something you want to have out with me?"

Fallon leaned back against her father's bureau and crossed her arms. "What a melodramatic question, Krystle. Really. Have what out?" She waited, but Krystle was waiting, too. "If it's that little talk I overheard—oh, all those months ago—between you and Matthew, at the party—has that been on your conscience all this time? Let's see; how did it go? 'Hate you? I don't hate you, Krystle, I love you!' And something about if you had known he felt that way, you wouldn't have—something or other—well, come on, Krystle! That was a party, and we all say things at parties. I mean, if I ever got quoted after two sips of champagne—is that what you mean? Or was there something else? Have what out, Krystle?"

The silence was long and tense.

Then Fallon stuck her hands in her jeans pockets and shrugged and left the room. Krystle stood there for a long time, staring down at the black box in her hand.

She was roused out of her painful reverie by the telephone buzzing on the little table nearby. She shook her head to clear it and picked up the receiver.

"A call for you, Mrs. Carrington. He wouldn't give his

name but said you would take the call. Do you want me
to hang up on him?"

"No, thank you, Mary. It's all right. Hello?"

"Krystle, it's Matthew. I hope you don't mind my
calling you at home; thought it best not to advertise—"

"It's all right, Matthew. You sound excited."

"I sure am! The well's in, Krystle—came in last
night, a real gusher! It's pumping faster and richer than
even Walter anticipated! We made it, Krystle. It's in!"

"Oh, Matthew, I'm so glad!"

"I had to tell you first. It was thanks to you, you
know."

"No. That's not true at all. You're the one who did it,
you and Walter. I only lent you a Band-Aid when you
got scratched."

"Krystle, I can pay you back now. As soon as the
assay goes through and the bank gets its piece off the
top—shouldn't be more than a few days, week at the
most. All right?"

"Yes, fine, fine, Matthew."

"Good. See you, then."

"Yes, see you."

As soon as she had hung up, the telephone rang
again. This time it was Blake, with the same news. His
voice was remote and controlled, barely covering his
angry rage.

"I'll be home for lunch," he said. "I want something
light to eat and some quiet time with you before I go
back to the office."

And a few drinks, she knew. Blake had fallen into the
habit of coming home for lunch when he wanted to
drink more than he wanted his business associates to be
aware of. It was true that he sometimes had other

reasons for coming home in the middle of a busy day—to talk with her or to make love to her, sometimes. But she had a feeling that today would not be one of those.

He didn't bother to conceal his rage. "Somebody bailed Blaisdel and Lankershim out," he fumed as he downed his third scotch on the rocks. Krystle toyed with her salmon mousse and listened to him carefully. "They fished out that bit and kept on going and hit it, hit it big, too. I want to know who gave them the money, and I intend to find out."

"Why, Blake? What difference can it make now?" she asked a little fearfully.

"Because I can't tolerate betrayal, that's why. I have suspicions—somebody went behind my back, and that somebody could be Patrick or Harrison or MacReady or Manning or even Colby. I won't rest 'til I know who it was."

"But they're your friends, Blake. It wasn't one of them."

He looked at her over the rim of his glass. His eyes narrowed. "How do you know?" he asked.

"I—I know them. I can feel it."

He drained the glass and poured himself another from the decanter set into the ice bucket. He held the frosty glass in both hands and turned it as he talked.

"My friends. Krystle, let me tell you something about my friends. In this business, the only friend is a dead enemy. Friends! The minute you're on the ground, these friends will attack you like a pack of hungry dogs."

Troubled, Krystle shook her head. "Why do you say that?"

Blake smiled thinly. "Because I'd do the same to them if the situation were reversed. Hey, you're trembling. Too late in the season to sit outside, I guess. Shall I call for a sweater?"

"No, it's not that. I—I just don't like seeing you upset."

Blake sipped his drink. "How about Matthew getting his strike? Don't you enjoy seeing him on top? As I recall, you were always one of his cheerleaders—a staunch supporter. You must be secretly cheering now that he's made a touchdown. Loyally, though, you're not showing it. At least not to me." He drained the glass.

"Blake," Krystle said slowly, seriously, trying to reach him before it all went much too far, "why are you making an issue of Matthew? I mean, you have so much. Why did you want to crush him? For a well you didn't need?" When there was no answer, she went on. "What I feel about Matthew is happy for him, for his family, for his crew's families. Just happy that they're getting their chance."

Blake stared at her for a long moment before answering. "I admire your humanitarian concern. I mean that, Krystle. It's one of the things that attracted me to you from the beginning," he said, sincerely if a bit unsteadily. "A talent you have, something I've envied at times."

"I've seen you act with compassion, Blake, when people least expected it," she said softly. "You're not always the Caligula you sometimes pretend to be. See? I happen to know you very well."

"The real Blake Carrington." He grunted, smiling a little lopsidedly.

"The Blake I fell in love with and married," she agreed.

They were holding hands when the terrace door flew open and Fallon appeared. "Hi, everybody. I just had lunch with Peggy at the club. Everyone's buzzing about the well coming in for Blaisdel and Lankersheim. I guess you heard, huh? My, don't you two look cozy. May I join you, or is this strictly a twosome?"

"The message is lousy, but the messenger's kind of cute," Blake said. "You may stay."

Fallon plopped herself down between them. She reached for her father's glass and took a swallow. She shuddered with the taste of it and then took another sip.

"Wonder where they got the money to repair that bit," she mused out loud.

"You know anything, missy?" Blake asked sharply.

Fallon sat back in her chair. "Let's go for a ride," she said restlessly. "How about it, Dad? A good fast canter? It's a great day for it."

"Just what I was thinking," Blake said, getting up from his chair.

"Sorry you don't ride well enough, Krystle," Fallon shot over her shoulder as she went inside to change. "Come on, Dad. Race you to the stables!"

Blake stopped to kiss Krystle's hand. "See you later," he said.

She clung to him for a moment. "Blake—"

"Yes?"

"Remember—I love you. I do."

Blake leaned down to brush his lips gently across her cheek. "A few more lessons and you'll be able to come with us," he assured her.

Krystle forced herself to smile and let him go.

Fallon led the way, as she had done ever since her first little Shetland pony, wherever impulse took her, through the thickets and woodlands of their mountain side. It was a cool, crisp day; the leaves were starting to turn blood red on the beautiful but deadly parasite vines that fed off the sturdy old oaks and hemlocks along the trail. Blake followed his daughter, the only person he would ever allow to lead him. He enjoyed the sight of her slim, proud back, the apparent ease with which she handled the willful stallion.

Arriving at the waterfall, their accustomed place for a break, Fallon threw herself down on the crinkly leaves cushioning the bank of the stream. Blake dismounted and walked over to the gentle water that tumbled over the rocky slope. He bent to take a drink with his cupped hands. Fallon called out to him.

"Something better in my saddlebag if you're interested!"

Blake straightened up, cocked his head at his daughter. He went to her horse, patted the smooth hide, and reached into the soft leather pouch. A flat silver flask, cold to the touch of his sweaty hand, proved to have been recently filled to the brim with scotch.

"I didn't know you'd taken up heavy drinking," he said.

"I haven't. I thought you might get thirsty. Just being the thoughtful daughter. Okay?"

He laughed and took a deep swallow. He screwed the silver cap on and tucked the flask back into her saddlebag. Then he thought better of it, took it out, and slipped it into his own jacket pocket.

"So how're things, Dad?" she asked casually.

"Great. Fine. Why do you ask?"

"Who do you suppose bailed Matthew Blaisdel out?"

"No idea. Yet." Blake hoisted himself onto the grass near her. They both watched the water tumbling over the rocks and listened to the soothing, gurgling sound that had always gone on and probably always would.

"It wasn't you, was it?" she asked innocently.

"Me? Why in hell's name would I do that? You know better than that, Fallon. Or I thought you did."

"Oh," she said. She reached for a thistle top and carefully pulled it from its sheath, stuck the clean, white, virginal shaft between her sharp white teeth, and chewed it.

"What made you ask me that?" Blake said, eying his daughter suspiciously.

"Well, Krystle offered to lend me her emerald to wear tonight. The minute I saw it, of course, I realized that it was a copy. You must have had it made and not told her, huh? Knowing she wouldn't know the diff—"

"Fallon Carrington, you'd better have a damned good explanation for what you're telling me. What in hell is this about?"

"Oh, my God. Don't tell me you didn't—oh, gosh, what have I let out of the bag—Dad? Daddy? I'm sorry. I just assumed you needed some cash real quick and—"

"And I hocked my wife's jewels?" Each word was an icicle sharp enough and cold enough to kill, but they were not aimed at Fallon, and she only trembled a little.

"Well, I knew somebody did. I knew the minute I saw them."

Blake swung up into his saddle. He turned his roan's head up from the sweet grass and back toward the house.

"Wait for me," Fallon said, scrambling to her feet.

He waited, holding the reins impatiently. Fallon was up and ready in a moment. "Fallon," he said in a troubled voice, "I don't have to tell you not to—"

"Not to say anything? Daddy, don't insult me by asking me that."

"There's my girl," he said, a bit too absent-mindedly for Fallon's taste. He flicked his heel against his mount's red flank and was off at a gallop. Fallon followed as best she could, but not even she could keep up with Blake Carrington when he was in a hurry.

10

Matthew Blaisdel stepped out of the Rolls-Royce (guaranteed by the dealer to be two feet longer than the custom job owned by Blake Carrington) and grinned down to see his weather-beaten old partner enjoying his new toy so much.

"Thanks for the lift, Walter. It was a real soft ride," he said as he stepped onto the curb in front of his own house. The Rolls door closed itself electronically, and soundlessly.

"I'm just testing it, you understand. Not sure I'm going to buy it yet," Walter said. He was leaning back against the soft chamois and puffing a vile-smelling cigar.

Matthew laughed. "Well, by the time the checks actually start rolling in, you'll probably have your mind pretty well made up," he commented with as straight a face as he could muster. Walter puffed on his cigar, touched a button, and the car moved like a giant ocean liner down the quiet suburban street.

When Matthew walked in, Claudia was on her knees in front of the fireplace in the living room, trying to fan a listless fire into something more cheery. When she turned around to greet him, there was a little smudge of soot on her nose. He found it oddly moving.

"Where's Lindsay?" he asked.

"Upstairs, doing her homework. I thought you and I could have a drink in front of the fire, only I can't seem to—"

"I'll get the fire going; you get the drinks."

When she came back, he had spread a handful of colorful travel brochures out on the cocktail table. She looked down at them and then over at him.

"Pick a card," he said, smiling.

"What are these, Matthew?" she asked.

"Well, I think if you look real hard, you'll see they're hotels, resorts, that sort of thing." Matthew was not very good at this, and he felt awkward. That only made him realize how long it had been, how far apart he and Claudia had drifted in these last few years. It made him sad, and sorry. He leaned forward, pointing. "Look at them," he said, "and if you look real hard, you'll see that one of them—this one—is a place I used to hear you mention from time to time."

Claudia picked up the brochure he pointed to and looked through it quickly. She was almost in shock. "I only said that I heard it was beautiful," she said slowly.

"And what I heard you saying was that you wished we could go there someday. And well, now that the well has come in and we're going to be living easier, I think it's time you and I got to know each other again. Maybe take that honeymoon we never had. How about it?"

Claudia felt close to tears. She took a sip of her drink. "Matthew, I think we've passed that stage. I mean, honeymoons."

"I don't know—we never tried it. Look, I'm only talking about a weekend, anyway, for now. We don't really have the money yet, and I can't take any real time away, especially now, but it would be a start in the right direction, wouldn't it? What do you say?"

"What about Lindsay?"

"She can spend a couple of nights with my mother. I think they kind of miss each other, actually." Now that Matthew had decided to patch up their marriage—or give it a try, anyway—he couldn't understand why she wasn't showing more enthusiasm. Wasn't that exactly what she had been wanting all this time?

"My clothes," she said. "I don't have the right—"

Matthew picked up the brochure from the table where she had let it fall. "I read this thing," he said, "and it says—right here someplace, yes, here—'new management, informal atmosphere.' That means I won't have to wear a tie and you won't have to change four times a day." His determined smile was beginning to wear thin.

"Why do you really want to do this, Matthew?" Claudia asked softly.

He threw the brochure down. "Because there's something I want to—because I owe it to you, Claudia," he said finally and with absolute sincerity. "Because you deserve it. Because I've made mistakes. I've probably hurt you from time to time, and I don't want you to be hurt. And because I love you."

"Do you?" she whispered.

It was an almost imperceptible beat before he answered her. "I want to," he said honestly.

Her eyes did brim over then. "Okay," she agreed. When he kissed her, she tried not to think of Steven.

But the next day she was in Steven's arms, in his bed at the apartment on Kensington. He was telling her about his tree, the one he had planted when he was a little boy.

"It overlooks the prettiest point of the lake," he said. "Next spring, I want you to be up there with me when she starts to show off. The greenest leaves and the sweetest form of any tree anywhere in the world—hey, what's the matter? Don't be jealous of my tree. I love her, but I love you more. Claudia? What's wrong?"

She ran her hand through his long hair and pushed back the unruly cowlick and leaned up to kiss him. "Steven, I've been thinking, wondering how to say it. This has to be the last time for us."

He flinched as though he had been struck. But he didn't move away from her. "Don't you love me?" he asked.

Claudia let her hand caress his bare shoulders. "How can I not love you?"

"Then why? Why? Why?" He pressed himself to her and kissed her mouth so that she couldn't answer except with her body.

But later, when they were calm again and reasonable, they agreed to stop seeing each other, painful as it would be. As Matthew's wife, Claudia owed him the chance to save their marriage. As Matthew's friend, Steven would step aside. Loyalty can hurt as much as love, sometimes.

Steven was lonelier than he had ever been in his life after Claudia left. But pacing his little apartment and looking out on the lights of busy Kensington Street, he was glad to be there, on his own, rather than back in New York with a different kind of love. Or worse, in his father's house up on the mountainside. There were tensions in that house that were immeasurably worse than loneliness.

Blake Carrington was spending many hours and many evenings at the desk in his study, working alone. No one was allowed to disturb him. But one night, Krystle knocked on his door around nine o'clock. There was no answer at first, and then he called out, "Who is it?" He sounded annoyed.

"Mrs. Carrington," she said, and waited.

"I'm on the phone," he answered curtly. She pushed the door open, balancing the heavy tray with its heavy silver tureens keeping the food hot. "All right if I come in?" she asked, and without waiting for an answer, she crossed the room to set the tray down on top of the papers that were strewn on his desk.

He was talking with Mike Nuzzi, the computer expert, about installing a two-and-a-half-million-dollar system throughout all his offices and connecting branches around the world. It was a complicated discussion, and Krystle waited patiently, listening with keen interest to the one side of the conversation she could hear. She felt a twinge of real regret that she was no longer involved in his business life. Or her own, for that matter. Mr. Nuzzi said something funny, and Blake laughed over the phone, but when he hung up and turned to Krystle, all trace of amusement had vanished. He looked at the tray on his desk.

"I'm not hungry," he said. "I thought I had made that clear."

"You've got to have something, Blake," she said, trying to smile him out of his mood.

He didn't answer, but seemed to be waiting for her to

leave. They were both standing. He wasn't even looking at her. "Hey," she said softly, "am I complaining that I've had to sit in that dining room alone the past couple of days?"

"Fallon and Jeff ought to be back from Paris in a day or two," he said.

Krystle kept her smile and her patience. "It's not Fallon or Jeff I'm missing," she said. "It's you."

Finally, he looked at her and visibly softened. "I've been so—I have deserted you, haven't I?"

"Yes, a little," she said. "I mean, you've been here, but you've cut yourself off. I just wish I knew why."

She touched his face.

"I'm very pressured," he said, looking at the desk.

"I know. But it's not healthy," she said. She dropped her hand.

"I feel fine."

She looked at him with a wry smile. "You don't look fine. Handsome, yes, always. But fine, no. Too much work, not enough relaxation. Blake, Wednesday is Cecil Colby's birthday."

"So?"

"Well, I thought we should give him a party. He's Jeff's uncle and your closest friend. He lent you money when you needed it, helped bail you out—"

"People do that for one reason and only one," Blake cut in fiercely. "To make the recipient of the loan beholden, that's why. Cecil Colby thinks I owe him something. And for that you think I should give him a party."

"Blake—"

"Forget it." He moved around and sat back down at his desk, as if dismissing her.

"But Blake, it's family. Jeff and Fallon will be home and—"

"Forget it, Krystle," he said sharply. "I don't need a damned party. And I wish you'd leave me alone. Is that clear enough?"

Puzzled and hurt, she managed to hold on to her own temper because of her concern for him. "Blake, why are you being so sharp with me?" she asked quietly.

He looked up. Then he shot his words like bullets at her. "Have you been faithful to me?"

She clenched her fists until the fingernails cut into her flesh. Her eyes locked with his until finally she trusted herself to answer. "If I told you the truth," she said, "would you believe me?"

Stalemate. They stared at each other miserably, with no place to go. Krystle broke the anguished silence.

"You're not an easy man to live with, Blake."

"So I've been told," he answered coldly. She turned to leave, but he stopped her with another question. "Is there something you want to tell me?"

"You mean a confession?" she asked sadly. "Do I have anything to confess?"

His stern silence said that was exactly what he was asking.

Krystle could only whisper her answer. "No—no, I don't."

Determined not to cry, she left the room and went upstairs. She soaked for a long time in the whirlpool tub, listening to Mozart on the stereo, and then she got into bed with a good novel to read. Blake had been sleeping in a guest room the past few nights, saying that he didn't want to disturb her sleep after working late, and so she was startled when he came in shortly before midnight.

"Krystle, I've been thinking about what you said. And I've changed my mind. We should have a party for Cecil; of course we should. It's a wonderful idea. Will you make the arrangements? His favorite restaurant is the Chambiges. It's in New Orleans. Invite the whole family—Jeff and Fallon and Steven and even Steven's girl, if he's really got one."

"Oh, Blake, that's wonderful. I'm so glad you decided—"

"I'd like you to do something else for me," he cut in as he started to unbutton his shirt. He said it almost as an afterthought. "I'd like you to wear the emerald necklace that evening."

He wasn't looking at her, and if she turned suddenly pale, he did not notice. "Will you do that for me?" he asked, pausing on the threshold of the dressing room and waiting for her answer.

Not trusting herself to speak, she nodded, and he seemed contented with that for an answer.

She knew that Matthew would pay her back at the very first moment he could. She could not, would not, ask for the repayment of her loan. The six months were not quite up yet; there was time. Only not for her, it seemed.

She deliberately chose a dress that would not look right with the emerald on its gold chain—a dark-blue silk with a lace collar, low-cut and more appropriate with a simple strand of pearls. She was shocked to see her hand trembling as she fastened the luminescent pearls around her neck.

"I asked you to wear the emerald," Blake said. She hadn't noticed him standing behind her. Their eyes met in the mirror.

"I thought the pearls would look better with this dress," she said.

"They might," he agreed pleasantly. Krystle felt relief wash over her so violently that it made her weak, but almost instantly the tension froze her again. Blake had walked over to the wall safe and was spinning the combination lock. He reached inside for the black box and held it out to her. "But I'd like to see the emerald on you one last time," he said.

"I don't understand," she said in a small voice.

He opened the box himself and took out the huge green stone, letting the chain dangle from his hand. With his other hand, he touched Krystle's pale cheek, running his finger softly across the high, prominent arch of her cheekbone. Then he began to fasten the necklace around her throat.

"You've always said that if there were any way you could help me, you would do it," he said softly. His hands were huge and warm against her skin. She could only nod, watching his reflection in the mirror.

"I've been regrouping, selling off corporations. Mike Nuzzi is giving me an incredible deal on the computers— the man's a genius, and he's helping me enormously, but still, I've got to get hold of quite a bit of cash right away. The money I can get for this necklace won't be much, but it might help a bit. And you haven't been wearing it much. You won't miss it, will you?"

He kissed the top of her head and left the room. Krystle felt a chill run down through her whole body.

The green stone hung around her neck like a hundred-pound block of ice.

In their room just down the hall, Jeff and Fallon were dressing for the party, too. He came out of the shower with a towel around his waist and caught his breath sharply at the sight of her in her slip, leaning forward to apply eye makeup, concentrating so hard that the tip of her pink tongue peeked between her teeth. He went to her and lifted her bodily from the chair in a great warm and loving surge of passion.

"What are you doing, Jeff!"

"What does it feel like I'm doing?" he said, laughing. He set her down on the bed and started to embrace her again, but she pushed him away.

"We've got to get dressed," she said.

"I'm the fastest dresser in the West," he said, "and we've got a good half hour."

"I've got my makeup on," she said. She sat up and started to get off the bed, but he stopped her with his outstretched hand.

"You can fix your makeup."

She pulled away. "Jeff, we're going to a party for your uncle, and—"

"And he wouldn't mind. Believe me; in fact, I think he'd prefer it if we stayed here and—you know." He tried to pull her down again, to kiss her, but she pushed him off and went back to her dressing table.

He stared at her. "Why did you marry me?" he asked with an unexpectedly hard edge to his voice that she had never heard before.

She tried to kid it away. "I could have done worse. You're pretty good-looking," she said.

"So are a lot of guys," he answered, still waiting for her answer.

"You're rich," she said flippantly.

"Not so rich as you."

"What can I tell you?" she shrugged. "You're kind to orphans."

Jeff was off the bed and at her side, turning her toward him so hard that his fingers were making marks in her arm. "I asked you a question," he said. "Why did you marry me?"

"Will you please stop being dumb and get your clothes on?" she snapped back.

"You don't have the nerve to tell me, do you?" He sneered. He walked away from her and started to dress.

Fallon could never ignore any kind of challenge. "Oh, don't I?"

He ignored her, making her really furious. "Okay, Jeff, you want to know? Here it is. I married you because I made a deal with the devil, and I wish to God I hadn't."

He stared at her. "What kind of deal?" he asked.

But Fallon was already sorry she had said it. "Nothing. Forget it," she said. She threw down the mascara brush and turned to go past him, but Jeff grabbed her wrists with both hands and made her look at him.

"What kind of deal?" he growled intensely.

"Let go of me."

"WHAT KIND OF DEAL?"

Through clenched teeth, Fallon spat at him, "I married you because your uncle promised to bail out my father if I did!"

Jeff's hands dropped from her. He stared at her in disbelief. Slowly, he turned away from her and caught hold of the foot post of their bed, leaning against it. He stared off into nowhere as though trying to fathom what she had said.

Frightened, rubbing her wrists, Fallon took a step or two toward him. "Hey, Jeff, c'mon. You know that's not true. I just made that up because you got me mad. I just made the whole thing up. Okay? C'mon, Jeff."

He looked at her, and what she saw in his eyes made her smile fade again. She stepped back. He shook his head as though to clear it and then moved toward his bureau.

"What are you going to do?" Fallon asked nervously.

"I'm going to get dressed," he said coldly. "We have my uncle's birthday party to go to."

Eight cheerful celebrants stepped off Blake Carrington's private plane in New Orleans that night. In addition to Jeff and Fallon, Blake and Krystle, Andrew Laird and his wife, Emily, came along, and Cecil Colby brought a date, a young woman named Bethany, who wore a great deal of makeup and a very short skirt. They had been drinking and toasting all the way from Denver, but even a casual observer would have noticed some vague and undefined tensions beneath the forced gaiety of the party.

The two limousines pulled up in front of the restaurant, amd the owner rushed out to greet them, to hold the door open, to make a fuss over them. It made them the center of all attention for a while. The excessive drinking that Jeff Colby was doing soon made them even more of an attraction to the other diners. During the meal, he kept his uncle's date busy on the dance floor, and as the evening progressed, his dancing became wilder, his hands on Bethany's bare back more possessive, his laughter louder, and his ability to drink and dance at the same time more precarious.

At the table, Blake was quietly drinking more than he should, too. Krystle was at the opposite end of the table, trying to make polite conversation with Emily Laird and Cecil Colby. She was conscious every second of the terrible weight of the emerald around her neck. The false cheer that had contained the group on the plane and during the first part of the meal now seemed to fall away of its own heavy weight. Finally, no one made much attempt to do anything but stare at Jeff Colby's antics with Cecil Colby's girl.

Suddenly, Blake turned to Fallon. "Can't you do something about your husband's behavior?" he snapped.

She shrugged. "You do something," she said carelessly. "You picked him out for me, remember? If you don't like the way he behaves, you tell him. Or have him beat up or something."

Blake glanced over at the dance floor again. Jeff was throwing a twenty-dollar bill on a waiter's tray and removing two filled glasses from it for himself and Bethany while pressing his body as close to hers as he could manage without falling over. "At the moment," Blake muttered, "that doesn't seem like such an altogether bad idea."

He looked across at Cecil, who was clearly furious but pretending not to be. Andrew and Emily Laird were dancing, more to keep out of the coming explosion than because they couldn't resist the music, Blake suspected.

The waiter put another drink in front of Blake, and he downed it in one gulp. He glowered at Fallon, who was watching the scene as if she had paid for a ticket. At the opposite end of the table, his exquisite wife sat tense and alone, thinking her own thoughts and just as glad that people were looking at Jeff instead of at her.

The music stopped, and Jeff shouted, "Play it again!" and started digging in his pocket for another bill, not relinquishing his sweaty hold on giggling Bethany.

"Jeff! Bethany, will you join us? I believe it's time to toast Cecil on his birthday," Blake called out in a tone that was not to be ignored or disobeyed.

The two giddy young people stumbled their way, laughing and almost falling, back to the table. They stood there, holding their drinks and holding each other up.

Blake raised his glass.

"To you, Cecil. You've been a good friend. And more. I don't think it's any secret at this table that you helped me out of some small difficulty recently—"

"And all it cost you was your daughter," Jeff Colby put in loudly. "A real bargain." He swayed toward Blake and would have fallen but for his uncle, who rose from his chair and grabbed his arm.

"You sit down now, Jeff, before you make a bigger fool of yourself than you already have," Cecil ordered with quiet fury.

Jeff giggled. "I'd love to, Uncle Cece, but I can't. You know me—dancing feet, soul of a gypsy, good-time Jeffie, everybody's boy, always smiling, always dancing— ta-da—" He tried to execute a little dance step.

Bethany spoke up. She was totally oblivious to the tension in the group. "Hey, Cecil, your nephew is really some terrific dancer, you know that?" In the moment's embarrassed silence that followed, it got through

to her that she might be out of line. "I'm interrupting
something, right? I'm sorry." She managed to find her
lips with her forefinger and quieted herself like a
naughty but unrepentant child.

Jeff tightened his arm around her. "That's all right,
honey," he said. "Nobody minds. By the way, have you
met these folks? I mean, really met them—allow me."
He began moving with her alongside the table, unsteadily,
talking loudly. Around the room, other conversations
stopped as the restaurant's customers watched and listened
with fascination. The Carrington party could only wait
in stony silence for Jeff to play out his game.

"Cecil Colby you know, of course. Been called an
unprincipled con-glom-er-a-teur."

"What's that?" Bethany giggled, enjoying the limelight.

"Something he's very, very proud of," Jeff said. "And
you know, pride goeth before destruction." His voice
became confidential but still much, much too loud.
"Actually," he went on, "he's a white slaver. Buys and
sells people. So you look out for him, okay?" She
nodded as Jeff moved her along to Andrew Laird.

"That fella there, going a little thick around the
middle? Would you believe he was once one of the
most brilliant criminal attorneys in the Rocky Mountain
states? Gave up his career to shuffle papers for Blake
Carrington. At a scandalous salary, of course. But then
who am I to judge him when I've been bought for a
spoiled little girl's monkey-on-a-string. And I didn't
even cost as much as a new polo pony."

They moved on down to Blake, who sat at the head of
the table with as much dignity as he could muster.

"Blake Carrington I never did like very much," Jeff
said. "As a kid, he scared the hell out of me. And I sure

wasn't real anxious to have him for a father-in-law. But I've got to confess—tonight I feel a little sorry for him. His drunken son-in-law has got the upper hand."

"Are you done, Jeff?" Blake said evenly.

"Not quite." He turned to Bethany again. "Seriously, though, folks, there is one here we really ought to drink to, and that's Krystle," he said, raising his glass toward the other end of the table. "She married into this diamond-studded zoo of ours without any preparation at all. And I've got a hunch she's the only one around here who can't be bought or sold. My god, who knows what price she's gonna have to pay for that! To you, Krystle! Good luck, kid. You're gonna need it."

Krystle stared at Jeff for a moment and then pushed herself away from the table and headed for a door at the rear of the restaurant. All she knew was that she had to get some fresh air.

Behind her, she heard Jeff say, "I'm done now. If there is anyone I haven't offended, please excuse me, but I've promised this young lady the next dance." He turned Bethany toward the dance floor, where the musicians had begun playing again.

The flight back to Denver was mostly silent. Jeff and Cecil's date had passed out cold; she was in the bedroom, and he was stretched out on one of the couches in the main cabin. Fallon sat flipping with exaggerated boredom through a magazine. Andrew Laird and his wife nodded on each other's shoulders on the other couch. Krystle curled up in an easy chair that was turned toward the window; she stared out at the glittering stars and kept her thoughts to herself.

When the "prepare for landing" buzzer sounded, Blake looked over at Cecil, who had been pretending to sleep. Their eyes met, and Blake raised an imaginary glass. "Happy birthday, Cecil," he said.

"Thank you." The two old friends and enemies both managed to find small, wry, philosophical smiles.

In the morning, as soon as Blake had left, Krystle got up and went to her safe. The black box was there, the emerald still inside it where she had placed it the night before. He had not taken it to sell, then, not yet. How long would she have to replace it? The telephone rang, jolting her from her preoccupation.

"Matthew! How nice to—sure, of course I will—Callie's Diner? Yes, I'll find it. In an hour? Yes, of course. See you there, then. Bye."

He was in a back booth, nursing a cup of coffee. "Thank you for coming," he said, standing up for her. She slid into the bench opposite him. He reached into his jacket pocket and retrieved a fat envelope, handing it to her.

She looked inside. The bills were crisp and new. "Thank you," she said.

"Thank me? Oh, Krystle, you'll never know how much difference it made. All the difference. We would have had to close down. I thank you for that."

Just as genuinely, Krystle nodded and said, "You'll never know how good your timing is."

Matthew turned to the counterman. "Two more coffees, please. Black for the lady."

Krystle smiled to realize that he still remembered how she drank her coffee.

"It's still a beautiful smile," he said. "But you're forcing it."

"Not the part of it that's seeing you," she said.

"What's wrong, Krystle?"

"Nothing—no, I can't lie to you. It's Blake. I'm worried for him. He's drinking too much and acting erratic. I don't know whether he knows I lent you the money or not. He seems almost to be my enemy these days, trying to trap me. Oh, God, I don't want to be disloyal. I shouldn't talk about him to you, behind his back. I'm sorry."

"You sound frightened."

Krystle started to shake her head, but she couldn't lie to Matthew. "I guess I am, a little," she confessed.

"You could leave him."

"No."

"Why not?"

"I did take vows, after all, and not that long ago. And I—I'm to blame, too. It's never just one person's fault, is it? Maybe I haven't been a very good wife. Haven't loved him enough."

All the pain and passion and deep, true love between them locked in their eyes for a moment like a naked embrace, but Krystle looked away quickly. Matthew got up to pay the check, and they got into their separate cars and went their separate ways.

She drove directly to Mr. Volkert's shop and parked nearby. When she pushed open the door, a Chinese bell tinkled over her head. In a moment or two, Mr. Volkert came out from his office in the back of the shop.

"Ah, Mrs. Carrington, yes," he greeted her. "Won't you come back into my office? More private, yes?"

She followed him behind the counter with its trays of jewels and antique artifacts locked behind musty glass. He offered her a chair. His office was neat and impeccably clean, in some contrast to the deliberately low-key, antique-store atmosphere of the shop. Here the serious, important business was conducted.

"I've brought the money to get back my necklace," she said, eager to get it over with. She opened her purse and took out the thick envelope Matthew had given her a half hour before.

"The necklace?" Mr. Volkert said with some surprise.

Krystle fought back a sudden panic. Her throat went dry. Surely he was not going to pretend that he never had it. "Yes," she repeated, "the emerald necklace."

Mr. Volkert sat down suddenly in the chair behind his desk. He looked stricken. "Mrs. Carrington, forgive me. But I never expected you to come back for it."

She swallowed hard and tried to stay calm. "What does that mean?" she asked.

"I have sold it."

Krystle couldn't, wouldn't believe her ears. "What?" she asked weakly. "Who to?"

He shook his head sadly. "A South American gentleman. Just a few days ago. I'm really so sorry, Mrs. Carrington. But if you read our contract carefully—"

She didn't hear the rest of his words. Somehow, she managed to stand up and leave his stuffy little office and to walk through the shop and down the street to her car. She found herself heading out of town, toward the turnoff on the bluff where she and Matthew used to meet. It was a place of good memories; she wanted to go there to feel comforted and to clear her head, to think about what she must do now.

But halfway there, she thought about what she had told Matthew, about her vows, about her own fallibility. That huge, unfriendly house perched on its own mountain side was where she belonged now. She couldn't run away from what she had done, what she must do. Her eyes dry and her mouth a little firmer than it had ever been, Krystle turned toward home.

11

Claudia and Matthew were shy together, almost like
real honeymooners. Other guests at the Breakers might
have mistaken their solicitous awareness of each other
and their avoidance of long silences for the tentative
new joy of lovers; in fact, they were two wary veterans
crossing a mine field, knowing too well the potential
dangers of each step. The resort was lovely, peaceful,
and romantic. There was nothing to do but be together,
dine well, lie on the beach, swim, look at the stars and
at each other. They began, carefully, to talk, to tell each
other their thoughts and hopes, to trust each other a
little bit again.

By Saturday night, at dinner overlooking the moonlit
sea, Claudia felt bold enough to bring up something
very important. "Matthew, do you suppose—do you
think there's any chance we could go someplace..."
She trailed off without finishing her sentence, not yet
certain enough to say what was on her mind without
some sign from him.

"Hey, I thought this was someplace," he said with a
little laugh. "And I thought you liked it. You want to
leave already? Where do you want to go?"

"No, it's wonderful here. I don't mean leave here; I
don't mean right now. I mean—well, permanently. Leave

Denver—move away, to another place, you and Lindsay and I."

"I don't get it, Claudia. What in hell—what are you talking about?" His automatic pilot put him on "angry," but he tried to check himself, to be understanding, to hear what she was saying.

"A fresh start, away from all the things and people in the past. That's what I want for us, Matthew. A fresh start."

"But we have a fresh start," he said. "The well is in, and we're going to make it big. I can't just take the money and run. I have a responsibility to Walter, and—"

"But suppose I asked you to do it for me," she said carefully, glancing at the moonlight outside the dining-hall window rather than at him. Then, because things were different now, she looked at him and took his hand. "What if I said it was important, very important for me, for our marriage? Would you do it?"

He looked worried now, with the old frown lines back in his forehead and alongside his mouth—had they ever really been gone? But she could not stop herself. If she and her husband still had a spark together, how could it be fanned into life while Steven still tempted her, while Krystle still hovered near Matthew?

"Matthew?"

"What is it you want to get away from?" he asked in his old, tired, and suspicious voice. She didn't answer. "Claudia, the last time we went through this it was demons and bats and people listening in on your conversations."

She took her hand out of his. Her voice was calm. "No," she said, "I'm not getting sick again, Matthew."

"Well, then," he said gently, "the answer is no. I don't think you're making any sense."

"Isn't it enough that I've asked you to do it? Isn't that enough?" she pleaded quietly.

Matthew didn't answer. He sipped at his wine. The food on both their plates was only half eaten. The honeymoon had lasted not quite a night and a day, she thought sadly.

"There's something you want to say, but you're not saying it," Matthew remarked finally.

Let's run far, far away from the Carringtons, she wanted to say. But— "It's nothing," she said. They finished their meal quietly and went upstairs. A truce, if not an understanding. They made love politely, like two old friends trying to discover what it was they had lost somewhere along the years.

The next morning, on the beach, Claudia rubbed his smooth, wide shoulders with tanning oil. Very casually, she said, "You know what, Matthew? Now that we can afford it, I'd like to take a course in word processing. I'm very eager to get a job as soon as I can."

"A job? What for? We're going to be pretty rich now. You don't have to work."

"I never did 'have to' work, did I? But I want to, Matthew. Please try to understand. I need something to look forward to every day—a challenge, and the sense of satisfaction when I can accomplish something on my own."

"I see."

"Do you?"

"I'm trying to. You're quite a girl, Claudia. I mean that."

"You mean I'm quite a woman," she said, smiling.

"Yes, that's exactly what I mean," Matthew agreed. He sat up, took the lotion bottle from her, and gestured with it that it was her turn to be massaged. She turned over and lay on the towel, the smooth sand under her cheek and his big gentle hands on her back, and she pretended that everything was all right. She had hoped that they could make it all right together. But if she had to do it on her own, she knew now that she could. She shut her eyes and listened to the waves breaking on the shore, each surge a new message, filled with life and its own momentum.

The weekend after Cecil Colby's birthday dinner was a time of tension in the Carrington mansion. Jeff and Fallon were alternately seen trying to kill each other at tennis or not speaking to each other around the house. Blake was closeted in his study the entire weekend. Krystle stayed quietly in her sitting room or the solarium, hoping her husband would come out and want to be with her. But it was like spending the weekend in a mausoleum, and by Monday morning Krystle was desperate for people, movement, a friendly smile, even from a stranger. She decided to do what most other rich women seemed to enjoy so much—go shopping. Fallon's birthday was approaching; she would try to find a gift for her.

Dressing quickly, she went downstairs and crossed the entrance hall to the front door. To her surprise, Blake came out of his study and met her in the hall with a warm smile.

"Good morning, Krystle."

"Good morning, Blake. I thought you'd have gone by now."

"Actually, I was waiting for you."

"For me?"

"Yes. I have some errands to run in town, and I'd like you to come with me. You weren't going anywhere that important, were you? Nothing that won't wait? You tell me that I don't spend enough time with you. Well, today's the day. And when we're finished with the errands, we can have a nice leisurely lunch wherever you'd like. All right?"

She nodded, puzzled but pleased.

Michael held the car door for them, and she got in. He seemed to know which way to go.

"Where are we going, Blake?" Krystle asked as the car turned toward the center of the city.

"Does it matter?" he asked her. "I thought it would be enough just to have time together. Look, the leaves have all turned already."

She said no more until they pulled up in front of Channing's, the jeweler's from whom Blake had bought her diamond earrings. She thought of that happy engagement shower with a pang—how long ago it seemed now.

"Channing's?" she asked. "What are we doing here?"

"I have a little errand," he said.

"Shall I wait for you?" she asked.

Blake shook his head. "Please come with me." Michael was waiting at the curb with the door open.

She got out and went with him into the elegant, hushed atmosphere of the store.

"Ah, Mr. Carrington, how nice to see you," old Mr. Channing said. They had been ushered into his private office by the store manager. Mr. Channing was very old, and semiretired, Krystle knew. He reputedly only came in to work when something or someone very special required his keen eye and accurate appraisal.

Krystle sat down on one of the deep velvet chairs that faced the Louis XIV table that served as Mr. Channing's desk. Blake reached into his jacket pocket and extracted Krystle's little black box. He handed it to Mr. Channing across the smoothly polished desk. The old man hefted it in his hand, looked at it admiringly, and said, "Very beautiful. Very."

Krystle was frozen. She could not move and would not have believed that she was even breathing. She felt lightheaded and wondered if she was going to faint for the first time in her life.

"I'd appreciate an appraisal, Mr. Channing," Blake said. "As quickly as possible. My wife isn't as fond of it as I had hoped."

"Of course," the old man said, smiling. He reached for a buzzer on his desk and pressed it. A thin, unsmiling young woman came in and took the emerald and its chain from Mr. Channing. She marched briskly out again with it.

"Well, now," Mr. Channing said, looking—rather sternly, she thought—at Krystle.

She braced herself. She had lied and was caught. Her husband would divorce her, of course, and she might even go to jail, she supposed. "What?" she had to ask. She had not heard the jeweler's words to her.

"I asked if you would like some coffee while we wait? My colleagues are simply verifying my own appraisal. It shouldn't take long. A cup of tea, perhaps?"

"No, thank you," she managed to say.

Mr. Channing and Blake talked about something; their words sounded very far away to her, and she didn't listen. In what seemed a very short time, the young woman marched in with the black box in her hand and a piece of paper, which she set down before Mr. Channing. He looked at it and cleared his throat.

"Well, now, you say you paid sixty thousand dollars for this, Mr. Carrington?"

"That's right," Blake said.

Can a husband send his wife to jail for selling his gifts to her? she wondered.

"May I ask where you purchased the stone?" Mr. Channing asked.

Maybe the jewels aren't really mine; I never did read that premarital agreement I signed. Maybe it said that expensive jewels would be only lent to me.

"From Beauvais," Blake was saying.

"Oh, yes. The best emerald man in the world. I see. . . ."

"Yes?"

I wonder if it's true that a scandal can ruin someone as big and important as Blake.

"Well, now," Mr. Channing was saying, "you got quite a bargain from him, I must tell you."

The room turned around and stopped. Krystle stared at the old man.

"Did I?" said Blake.

"Oh, yes, indeed. As an honest man, and if I've built my reputation on anything, it has been on honesty. Honesty—"

"What's it worth, Mr. Channing?" Blake interrupted. Like an overwound spring, Krystle leaned forward in her chair to catch the jeweler's words.

"Right now, as we speak, seventy-five thousand."

Blake's glance turned to Krystle, who clutched at the arms of the chair to keep the room from spinning.

"It's a magnificent stone, and perfectly cut," Mr. Channing said.

"Are you sure?" Krystle whispered.

Mr. Channing started to rear back as if insulted, but then he seemed to understand her and nodded reassuringly. "Well, it may be worth more to some, but I have to leave a margin for profit, you see."

"I see," Krystle said weakly.

"Darling, are you all right? You seem a bit upset?"

"No, I'm fine, Blake. Fine."

"Shall I have my cashier make out a check for you?" Mr. Channing asked.

Blake stood up and leaned over to take the emerald from the jeweler again. He weighed it in his hand, the chain dangling from between his fingers. "No," he said at last, "I believe my wife seems to be more partial to this piece than I thought she was. We'll keep it, after all. Thank you for your trouble, Mr. Channing."

He leaned over Krystle, opened her purse, and dropped the black box inside it. They said good-bye to Mr. Channing.

In the car, Krystle sat back against the cushions and closed her eyes. She heard Blake tell Michael to take them home, and then she heard the almost imperceptible sound of the glass between them and the driver sliding shut.

"You don't look well, Krystle. We'll go home instead of out to lunch, all right?"

She opened her eyes and looked at him. It was the same familiar, handsome face—kind, intelligent eyes, showing concern now; a tentative, worried smile on his lips; his perfectly cut hair framing sun-tanned, smooth-shaven cheeks; the little frown lines between his brows. It was not a lovable face, she thought.

"What is it, Krystle?" he asked.

She spoke without much emotion; it had all been drained out of her. "You set the whole thing up, didn't you? You've known about it all along—the necklace, the money, my loan to Matthew. You bought the real necklace back from Mr. Volkert, and then you made me go with you while you went through the charade of trying to sell it. Why did you do it, Blake? To humiliate me, to punish me?"

He sat back and stared straight ahead. The car was turning off the city streets onto the road leading up to their mountain. No sound could be heard from the highway traffic outside their soundproof cage.

"It's over now, Krystle," Blake said. "I believe you've learned your lesson. We can let it pass."

She had been wrong about her emotions; anger surged back through her with the full force of outrage. "What lesson, for God's sake?" she asked. "You may think I did something wrong. I don't!"

"Oh, I see," he said coldly. "And perhaps you'd like me to believe that Matthew Blaisdel should be a charity of mine, that he belongs somewhere between the Red Cross and Boys' Town."

"What is this obsession you have with destroying Matthew Blaisdel?" she cried out.

Working very hard to remain unruffled through this, Blake took a minute to compose himself. Then he said with infuriating superiority, "I told you, Krystle, this thing is over. Let it pass."

"It is not over. It will not be over until I sign some kind of affidavit that I am not sleeping with Matthew behind your back. Until I agree to be locked away in your castle like Rapunzel. Talk to no one, see no one. And only come out when you choose to display me on bank holidays and St. Valentine's Day."

Michael turned the car into their private drive, through the gates and up the long, sweeping curves toward the house. Blake sat in stony silence. Just before Michael opened the door for them, Krystle said softly, "I'm leaving you, Blake."

He waited politely for her to proceed him, out of the car and into the house. She paused inside the door, but he brushed past her and went toward his study. The butler closed the front door softly. Krystle stood there for a moment. The study door closed behind Blake. Krystle went, with heavy steps, to pack a very few things.

As she passed Fallon's room, she heard the sound of sobbing. Krystle stopped, wanting to knock on the door and go inside, to comfort and be comforted by another human being. But her unhappiness would be a victory for Fallon. Krystle kept on walking down the long corridor to her own room.

Fallon Carrington Colby was a young woman more accustomed to making other people cry than indulging in tears herself. She could almost always outthink other people, manipulate them and get her own way. On the very rare occasions when her imperious will came up against an immovable object, frustration and rage made her vulnerable and scared. Then the tears came, and she was a small, helpless child, truly terrified in a world she couldn't control. Her own husband, ever since his drunken display in New Orleans, had been acting as if she didn't exist. Or worse, didn't matter.

He hadn't gone to work this morning; when she'd asked why, he had stated as simply as he spat out anything he said to her any more, "I've quit."

"Quit! How can you quit? You're a Colby, the heir apparent to Colbyco, and you're Mr. Fallon Carrington, so you get the whole ball of wax someday from both sides. What do you mean, quit?"

He had ignored her. He was putting his toothpaste and razor and brushes in a little bag and the little bag in a bigger bag.

"You're full of it, aren't you," she had observed, and gone back to her magazine.

"I'm moving to New Orleans," he had said, closing the locks on his suitcase.

"Oh, yeah, you're a huge hit in New Orleans. They really loved your drunk act down there."

He didn't say anything.

"Jeff?"

"Yes."

"Are you really?"

"Yes."

"Well, what the hell am I supposed to do?"

"Get a divorce. Isn't that what you want?"

He waited for her answer. She stared at him and shook her head slowly. "I don't know. I haven't thought about it."

"Whatever you want, Fallon. Just let me know whenever you get ready." He started to leave.

"Jeff!"

"What."

"You can't just walk out on me like that!"

He shrugged and put his hand on the doorknob.

"Wait, Jeff!"

He waited.

Suddenly, she was terrified, trembling and crying huge salty tears that ran down her cheeks and made the tendrils of her hair wet. Her nose was stuffy, and she sniffed. Jeff was looking at her with no particular sign of interest in the unusual waterworks display. Fallon was scared.

"Don't leave me, Jeff, please!"

Astonishment registered across his face. He set the suitcase down but held his ground at the door, ready to walk out. He waited.

Fallon couldn't stop the crying and sniffling, and she felt like a perfect idiot. She reached for a tissue and made a stab at wiping her face. "I—I don't want you to leave, Jeff. You can't just leave, just like that. After all, we're married."

"Under false pretenses," he said bitterly.

"But I don't want you to leave!" she repeated helplessly.

"You don't want. I see. This is still about what Fallon wants, isn't it?"

She got up from the chair and moved toward him, stopped before she got very close. "You want it, too. I know you do, Jeff. You want to stay married, don't you? I know you love me, and I—I'll try to love you, honest I will, Jeff, only please don't go."

He couldn't resist her, of course. He opened his arms, and she flew into them and got his shirt all wet with her tears. But in a moment the shirt was thrown down on the floor along with the rest of their clothes, and it didn't matter at all.

Krystle was rereading the letter she had just written:

"I've loved you, Blake; I've loved you the best way I know how. But I guess that just isn't good enough.

"I know you've loved me, too, in your own way. But you frighten me, Blake. You're so many different people—gentle and sensitive one minute, treacherous and brutal the next. Maybe you need to be that way to survive in your world, but I can't live with the suspicion. I can't live with the rage. I love you, Blake, but I just can't live with you. Krystle."

She sealed the letter inside the blue envelope with her monogram on it. She propped it up against the lamp on Blake's side of the bed, and then she took the emerald out of its box and placed it in front of the envelope. It shone like a glorious and evil green sun. She turned away from it and went to the chaise longue to close the lid of her suitcase.

There was a perfunctory knock on the bedroom door, and before she could answer, it was pushed open to frame the major-domo and the butler, supporting Blake's limp body between them.

"Blake!" she exclaimed, running to him. "Is he sick? Did something happen?"

"No, Mrs. Carrington. He'll be all right. We just need to get him to his bed," Joseph said. She stepped back and let the two men half lead, half carry Blake into the room.

"He's drunk," she said with more relief than censure.

"Yes, ma'am," Edward agreed. Joseph shot a disapproving look at the butler, who was immediately and obviously sorry he had spoken at all.

"Thank you, Edward," Krystle said. "Thank you, Joseph. That will be all. I'll take care of him now."

Joseph looked pointedly at her open, filled suitcase. "That will be all, Joseph," she repeated sternly.

On the bed, Blake mumbled something unintelligible and then called out for Joseph. The major-domo went to him immediately, ignoring Krystle, who had to stand aside to let him pass.

"Yes, sir, Mr. Carrington?" Joseph said, bending over Blake.

Blake pulled on Joseph's striped tie and brought the haughty face down close to his own. Then he spoke, loudly and clearly. "I really love her, Joseph. I really do." With that, he fell back onto the pillow, and his eyes closed.

"Please go now," Krystle said quietly.

"But I know exactly how to take care of him now, better than you do, Mrs. Carrington, and it seems evident that you were on your way somewhere? I shouldn't wish to detain you—"

"Joseph, I am the mistress of this house. You work for me, and you will do exactly as I say the instant I say it. Is that clear enough?"

Edward backed out of the open door and went noiselessly down the hall. Joseph stood his ground at Blake's bedside. "I belong here, Mrs. Carrington. He needs me." *More than he needs you* was the clear implication.

Krystle went to the door and held on to the knob, out of patience. "Get out," she said. "Right now."

Joseph looked down at Blake, who had begun to snore. He looked back at Krystle, who met his stare head-on. His capitulation was brief and characteristically proud—a single, curt nod, and then he swept past her and out of the room. She shut the door.

She undressed him and got him under the covers. Then she tore up her letter, put the emerald in the safe, and began to unpack her bag.

ABOUT THE AUTHOR

EILEEN LOTTMAN is the author of six original novels and ten novels based on movies and television. *The Brahmins* was published in hardcover in the summer of '82 and will be available in paperback in March '84.

Some of Ms. Lottman's books include *Rich and Famous*, *The Greek Tycoon*, *After the Wind*, *The Package* and *The Bionic Woman* series.

Under the pen name of Jessica Evans, she has written books for young people including *Blind Sunday*.

Ms. Lottman is currently working on a musical adaptation of her novel, *Summersea*, for the stage.

DON'T MISS
THESE CURRENT
Bantam Bestsellers

☐	23481	**THE VALLEY OF HORSES** Jean M. Auel	$4.50
☐	23670	**WHAT ABOUT THE BABY?** Clare McNally	$2.95
☐	22775	**CLAN OF THE CAVE BEAR** Jean M. Auel	$3.95
☐	23302	**WORLDLY GOODS** Michael Korda	$3.95
☐	23353	**MADONNA RED** James Carroll	$3.95
☐	23105	**NO COMEBACKS** F. Forsyth	$3.50
☐	23291	**JERICHO** A. Costello	$3.95
☐	23187	**THE TOMBSTONE CIPHER** Ib Melchoir	$3.50
☐	22929	**SCORPION EAST** J. Morgulas	$3.50
☐	22926	**ROCKABYE** Laird Koenig	$3.25
☐	22913	**HARLEQUIN** Morris West	$3.50
☐	22838	**TRADITIONS** Alan Ebert w/ Janice Rotchstein	$3.95
☐	22866	**PACIFIC VORTEX** Clive Cussler	$3.95
☐	22520	**GHOST LIGHT** Clare McNally	$2.95
☐	22656	**NO TIME FOR TEARS** Cynthia Freeman	$3.95
☐	22580	**PEACE BREAKS OUT** John Knowles	$2.95
☐	20922	**SHADOW OF CAIN** Vincent Bugliosi & Ken Hurwitz	$3.95
☐	20822	**THE GLITTER DOME** Joseph Wambaugh	$3.95
☐	20924	**THE PEOPLE'S ALMANAC 3** Wallechinsky & Wallace	$4.50
☐	20662	**THE CLOWNS OF GOD** Morris West	$3.95
☐	20181	**CHALLENGE (Spirit of America!)** Charles Whited	$3.50

Prices and availability subject to change without notice.

Buy them at your local bookstore or use this handy coupon for ordering:

Bantam Books, Inc., Dept. FB, 414 East Golf Road, Des Plaines, Ill. 60016

Please send me the books I have checked above. I am enclosing $_____
(please add $1.25 to cover postage and handling). Send check or money order
—no cash or C.O.D.'s please.

Mr/Mrs/Miss_____

Address_____

City_____ State/Zip_____

FB—9/83

Please allow four to six weeks for delivery. This offer expires 3/84.